Battered to Death

Battered to Death

A Finch & Fischer Mystery

J New

Cover Illustration: William Webb
Interior Formatting: Alt 19 Creative

Remembering my girl Floss.
29th September 2008 to 14th June 2021

Missed every day.

OTHER BOOKS BY J. NEW

One

The beginning of summer in Hampsworthy Downs was as perfect as anywhere on earth could be as far as Penny Finch, mobile librarian, was concerned. The palpable warmth of sun on skin after its weaker rays over spring was a tonic for body and soul. The warm breeze blowing over the hills and fields brought with it occasional light rain showers ensuring the rolling green hills never turned brown, and watered the crops, thereby securing a good harvest for the farmers.

The air was filled with the fresh smell of earth and newly mowed grass as Penny pulled the door of her cottage shut, ready to begin her day. The door knocker tapped gently, causing Fischer, her rescued Jack Russell terrier, to let out an excited bark. He was as eager to start the day as Penny was.

Droplets of dew glistened on the camper van like diamonds as the bright morning sunshine scattered its rays over the village. Penny loved the old van, but it was much more than a simple vehicle. With the help of her dad she had converted it into a mobile library, a much needed resource for the villages and hamlets of the downs, and a lifeline for the elderly who rarely ventured to the main library in Winstoke town. Ready stocked with books in every conceivable fiction genre and reference books on almost any topic her customers could name, it held promises of romance, adventure and travel to other worlds. It really was a time-machine of sorts.

Penny unlocked the driver's door and felt her heart lift as she breathed in the intoxicating scent of books. Fischer let out an excited yip, his tail wagging furiously.

"In you get, Fish Face," Penny said and watched the little dog leap onto the driver's seat then gently step over to the passenger side, where he sat panting and smiling in anticipation. She climbed in with as much joy as Fischer and, turning the keys, brought the engine roaring to life.

Driving through the village of Cherrytree Downs never failed to lift Penny's spirits, and it was as much a pleasure today as it had always been. She had grown up here and never wanted to be anywhere else. She knew every stone, every corner, how the wind whistled around the memorial at the side of the road junction. Where the swallows built their nests and the best time to watch the young broods fledge. Some people may feel trapped in such a small place, but Penny loved every inch of it. Even Monday mornings felt like the first day of a holiday, especially in a job such as hers.

Penny glanced up at Sugar Hill on her right while Fischer was enthralled at the views outside his window. The two miles from Cherrytree Downs to Rowan Downs, her first stop of the day, was a beautiful drive with periodic glimpses of the sun sparkling on the river Switch and the hedgerows swarming with the little birds. She even spotted several rabbits hopping about in the fields, and if the barks were anything to go by, so did Fischer. Out of the corner of her eye she spotted a red kite circling lazily high overhead, riding the thermals rising from Sugar Hill. Penny slowed down and pulled over into a lay-by. She still had plenty of time to enjoy this rare sight.

"Mr Kelly will want to know about the red kite, don't you think, Fischer?" Pulling a notebook and pen from the glove compartment, she jotted down the time and location of the magnificent bird of prey. They were still rare, although now off the endangered list and slowing returning to their ancient habitats. This bird could be the one that had started nesting in the area last summer, now out hunting to feed her latest brood.

Penny flipped back through the pages of her notebook. Her latest scribbles were a mixture of animal sightings, book recommendations and a note to try rice milk. That one had been scribbled out. As a vegetarian any dairy alternatives were always tried, but she hadn't taken to this one at all. A few pages back she saw several notes reminding her that even in this most serene setting there was an occasional dark side. They pertained to two local murders she'd become involved in. The first at Christmas and the other not long into the new year.

She snapped the book shut not wanting to spoil the day with such sombre thoughts, and put it away as Fischer stood and put his paws on the dashboard, ears upright and alert as he watched the red kite circle overhead. He cocked his head quizzically and stared motionless as it suddenly spotted movement and dived, swooping down on its unsuspecting prey hidden in the tall grasses below. Penny scratched his ears and he stepped onto her knee, putting his paws on the steering wheel. She loved this little character and took a moment to let him know. He responded with a lick of her nose.

The bird swept away east towards her nesting site at Cringle Wood where two or three hungry chicks would undoubtedly be waiting. Penny checked both the rear view and wing mirrors before pulling back out onto the road. They were quiet in this area, especially in the morning, but she was a careful driver and knew better than to take risks on these country lanes.

The village of Rowan Downs was wide awake and bathed in glorious sunshine when she drove in and parked in her usual spot to wait for her first customers of the week. She opened the double side doors of the library, revealing a clever system of shelving filled with books, and before she could finish her preparations, she spied her first customers advancing. Lillian Greaves and Harriet Ward were a pair of well-known characters in the village and were almost always seen together, meeting up regularly to chat and argue. If a day went by in Rowan Downs and Lillian and Harriet were not quarrelling over some issue, village legends said it was a sign the world was about to end.

"You won't like it, Lillian," Harriet said, hurrying ahead of her friend.

"I'm sure I know myself well enough to be my own judge, Harriet," Lillian replied, retaking the lead.

The elderly ladies barged their way to the library door. Penny knew better than to get in their way and stepped aside before she was trampled underfoot. As did Fischer, who tucked himself safely under the van.

"Good morning, Mrs Greaves, Mrs Ward."

"The new Lynda La Plante please, Penny," Mrs Greaves said before her friend could get her request in first.

They both wanted this book so badly because they had heard Penny mentioning it to another customer one day. Unfortunately she couldn't remember which of them had asked first, although it was probable they couldn't either. They were usually happy to grab any book that came to hand, providing it had a criminal enterprise at the heart of it.

In her best impersonation of a magician, Penny produced a pair of books which had been hidden from sight. "Ta da! Ladies, you have no idea what I had to do to get my hands on two copies of this book."

Penny had known the fuss she would have faced this morn-ing if she'd only arrived with one book, so had pulled as many favours as she could from her friends Emma and Sam at the main library to get two copies.

"You are an absolute dear," Mrs Ward said. She handed over her library card and took the book, slipping into her shopping bag before her friend could snatch it for herself.

"What would we do without you, Penny?" Mrs Greaves said as she tucked her own copy of the book away in an instant.

Penny watched them walk off together, bickering over some new topic. She was sure the only thing preserving their lifelong friendship beyond a shared love of brutal crime stories was their eagerness to continually argue. They would probably live long lives, providing they both insisted on having the last word.

Penny checked her notes to see who else was due to pick up specific orders. There was only one, Dorothy Walker, who lived at the back of Chips Ahoy, the popular fish and chip shop in the village. An additional note said she had gone away on a short break late on Sunday night and would be back late on Friday.

The usual steady stream of patrons kept Penny happily occupied all morning. Chatting about books to interested people was not really like having a job at all. No doubt if she hadn't become the local mobile librarian she would have found another way to travel between the villages and hamlets of Hampsworthy Downs to talk about books all day.

As the sun rose higher, the camper van became too warm so Penny grabbed one of the folding camping chairs and sat outside. Fischer was snoozing in the shade. With midday approaching, she guessed she had seen all her regulars until she saw the old gentleman Mr Gregory hurrying towards her. He had a late return in his hands, holding it aloft as he scurried forward.

"Almost missed you again, Penny," he said, half out of breath as he handed her the book. "There's just so much to do in the garden at the moment and I almost lost track of the time."

"Don't worry, Mr Gregory," Penny said, issuing the small fine. Mr Gregory paid with the exact change without question or hesitation. He knew, as did the other patrons, it was partly how the library kept going.

"I don't want to keep you, Penny. I know you have a schedule to keep."

"Take your time, Mr Gregory, a few extra minutes won't matter." The last thing she wanted to do was cut short a customer's browsing time.

Mr Gregory quickly selected a new book from the gardening section and stepped down from the van. A moment later he was on his way home, leaving Penny to close up ready to take Fischer on his walk.

"Come on, little man," she said, dangling his lead. But Fischer didn't move, simply looked at her with his big brown eyes while his head still rested on his paws.

"I know, Fischer, it's a hot day but you need your walk. We both do. You're getting a little plump, and I don't know why. I haven't changed your diet at all. The vet gave you a clean bill of health the other day so there's no excuse."

It had been a long winter filled with excitement. Penny had developed a reputation not just as the local librarian but as the woman who had solved two local murders. But between dashing about investigating while holding down a full-time job, she enjoyed nothing more than being cosy by the fire with a cup of tea, a good book and a freshly baked piece of chocolate sponge cake.

She'd always been a size or two bigger than the women on television, but as long as she was healthy and was careful not to have cake every day, she was able to maintain her curvy figure without tipping the scales too far. Fischer, on the other hand, had not had any extras. She didn't treat him more often than usual, although her mum was a devil for giving him treats, rewarding him for every new trick he learned. But none of that explained why her little dog was putting on weight.

"Come on, Fish Face, a couple of laps around the village and then on to our next stop," Penny said, clipping the lead to his harness and dragging the reluctant pooch from his hiding spot.

Walking through the village was more of a lunchtime stroll than a serious walk, and Penny decided to see if they could make it down to the river before it was time to leave for Chiddingborne. She glanced down at Fischer trotting alongside her, his former reluctance to leave his comfortable shady spot entirely replaced by an enthusiasm for new sights, sounds and smells. An enthusiasm one could only find in dogs. She was sure he was smiling.

"We'll walk these extra inches off in no time, won't we, boy?" she said.

Looking up, she saw a small crowd outside Chips Ahoy, the Rowan Downs fish and chip shop. It was lunch time and therefore not unusual to see a queue snaking out of the door. People would happily drive the few extra miles forgoing their local chippy in favour of this one, and the shop drew customers from as far away as Winstoke as well as the nearby villages. There was something special about the recipe at Chips Ahoy that had made it quite famous.

Mr Sharp had run the shop for years, since Penny was a girl, it seemed. And during that time, the fish and chips had won several awards and had a reputation for being the best for miles around. Sadly, Mr Sharp had passed on several years ago and the shop had been taken over by his wife. She had maintained the excellent standard leading many to speculate it had been her all along who had been responsible for their special quality and flavour.

But Mrs Sharp lived up to her name. She was a grumpy, taciturn old woman, and it was clear why her jovial husband had fronted the business. Rowan Downs had lost a great local character when he'd passed away.

Fischer started to tug at his lead in a frenzy as they neared the shop.

"No, Fischer, we're not stopping I'm afraid," she said, trying to steer him in the direction of the river. As she came closer, she spotted the police car on the far side of the crowd, a panda car that was possibly the oldest constabulary vehicle anywhere in the country. It belonged to PC Bolton. Penny knew he liked a bag of chips as much as anyone, but close to retirement now it was rare to see him out and about these days. He seemed to spend much of his time in front of his police house, uniform jacket hanging on a garden fork stuck in the ground, his shirt sleeves rolled up, pot belly pushing aside his braces and glasses perched on the end of his nose as he studied his roses.

But there was something about the small gathering that felt wrong. This was not a happy queue of people waiting for their lunch, there was a murmur of concern rippling through the crowd. Lillian Greaves and Harriet Ward were standing together just on the edge of the main group, unsurprisingly engaged in an argument.

"She slipped on the grease I expect," Mrs Greaves said.

"Mrs Sharp knows her way around a kitchen," Mrs Ward countered. "And she's far too clean and tidy to have grease on the floor, Lillian, as you well know. You could eat her food off that shop floor. She's probably just had a funny turn. Hardly surprising at her age."

"Is everything all right?" Penny asked as she moved next to them.

"I'm afraid not, dear." Mrs Greaves replied. "Poor old Olive Sharp has had a fall. Someone found her lying in the back. Batter all over the place, they said. She probably slipped."

"So you say," Mrs Ward said, bristling. "She was as careful and sure-footed as you or I, Lillian."

"Oh dear, I hope she's all right," Penny said, wondering just how sure-footed Mrs Sharp really was. She'd only ever seen her standing at the long stainless steel shop counter. By contrast, she regularly saw Mrs Greaves and Mrs Ward positively charging around the village together like a couple of spring lambs despite their advanced years.

She heard a mumbled voice behind her say, "I can't understand what all the fuss is about. There are much better fish and chips to be found in Winstoke. Besides that, Chips Ahoy is an absolute eyesore in such a lovely village. It should be bulldozed and something better built in my opinion."

Penny turned round and found the speaker was a tall man in a rumpled brown suit with an unkempt ginger moustache talking to the woman next to him. He gave Penny a glare and sauntered away. The woman moved into the vacated space and the throng moved forward slightly.

A second younger man, smartly dressed in beige chinos and a casual but obviously expensive jacket echoed the sentiments of the unkempt man, then he too wandered away to be lost in the crowd.

Fischer was still agitated and straining at the lead to get to the shop. Sniffing the air in frenzy and whining, which was very unusual. Penny couldn't understand what had got into him. She pulled him closer and stroked his head in an effort to calm him. Then she felt her heart skip a beat, a sudden flutter that took her by surprise. Coming through from the back of the shop into the customer area was Detective

Inspector John Monroe. There was obviously more to this incident than a simple fall.

John Monroe and Penny had become friendly over the last few months after first meeting while Penny investigated the mysterious death of poor Mrs Montague. They'd not spoken for a while, and she berated herself now for her girlish response to seeing the tall, handsome detective inspector.

She and Fischer skirted around the crowd looking through the glass fronted shop and caught the DI just as he was leaving en route to his car.

"John," she said as she came alongside.

"Penny," he replied brightly. "How nice to see you. Hello Fischer," he added, bending to give the little dog a pat.

"Oh, Fischer, don't do that. I'm sure John can manage to clean his own shoes." Fischer was licking every inch of the DI's black brogues."

She gently pulled him away and walked with John to his car.

"What's happened in there? Is something the matter with Mrs Sharp?"

"And here I was thinking you just wanted the pleasure of my company."

"Oh, well yes, of course I do," Penny said.

Monroe smiled, happy to have teased her. Then he straightened up and the serious look was back. "You know I'm not able to discuss the details of a police investigation with you, Penny."

"So, it is a suspicious death?"

"Who told you that?" he asked, a bit sharply.

Penny gave a wry smile. "You just did," she said, returning the teasing.

Monroe let out a deep sigh. "That amateur detective's curiosity of yours will get you into trouble one day, Penny Finch."

"It's clear though, isn't it?" she said. "You don't need to be a detective to work it out."

"Clear is it? How so?"

PC Bolton stood in the doorway of the chip shop and held up his hands to the crowd, making sure there was space for a pair of police detectives to leave the shop unmolested. One was older and on the plump side, the other young, slim and much shorter. Both men wore crumpled shirts and ties fasten casually around unbuttoned collars.

"Yes, quite clear." Penny replied. "Why would a high ranking Detective Inspector be here otherwise? If it was something less serious then it would only be the local bobby taking notes. And possibly an ambulance. Which there isn't."

They both glanced over to PC Bolton, who was looking his usual disinterested self. He would probably be much happier at the station house with a cup of tea, munching his way through a packet of custard creams.

"Plus there are two Winstoke CID officers here."

Penny looked back at the shop as a white van pulled up and several forensic officers got out. Going to the rear of the

vehicle, they started to pull on white crime scene investigation overalls.

The silence of the crowd watching this new development
was deafening, and the enormity of it all suddenly hit Penny.

"Oh, poor Mrs Sharp." She looked up at John. "Was she
murdered, John? Is that what this is all about?"

Two

The Chips Ahoy premises had now been officially designated a crime scene. PC Bolton had run yellow crime scene tape across the open front door and moved the crowd back to a safer distance. Penny had her own work day to continue, as did Detective Inspector Monroe. They said goodbye, and Penny concluded her short walk with Fischer along the banks of the river before returning to her van. As she left Rowan Downs she saw one of the white overall wearing forensics' team lift the tape and exit the shop. She wondered what they'd found.

The countryside was bright and cheerful, filled with wild flowers and teeming with life, but Penny couldn't help but think about the tragedy which had struck in Rowan Downs. She felt her concentration drifting as she drove the familiar route to Chiddingborne. Driving on auto-pilot was as dangerous as driving blindfold her dad had once told her. She always remembered that no matter how familiar the roads between the villages were to her, the unexpected could happen at any moment. She shook her head, focusing on the road, and gave it the attention it deserved.

The red kite was once again circling overhead. Penny checked the small analogue clock on the dashboard, the numbers glowing bright green, she would be late if she stopped and pulled over to write it down now. She made a mental note instead and would add it to her notebook later.

The regular Chiddingborne customers were happy to see Penny as they always were, but several commented that Penny was not her usual cheerful self. She couldn't deny the death of Mrs Sharp had been a shock. She didn't patronise the chip shop, but it was as much a part of the village landscape as the chalk bed river, Sugar Hill and even her own cottage. Now, to see it reduced to a crime scene and devoid of life saddened her. She made no mention of the murder; the news had obviously not filtered over to Chiddingborne yet, but it wouldn't be long before the rumours and whispering started.

Penny brightened as the day continued, and the steady stream of library patrons engaged her in conversation. She found talking about books and the latest best seller or favourite read a comfort as well as a distraction. She lost herself in conversations several times over the course of the afternoon, but thoughts of Mrs Sharp were never far away and returned all too soon during quieter moments.

She thought too of John Monroe. Main subject matter withstanding, it had been a real pleasure to chat with him. She had got to know him reasonably well over the preceding months and knew him to be warm and friendly. Someone she could happily spend time with. She felt at ease in his presence and looked forward to seeing him again.

With the afternoon coming to an end and with all her regular customers dealt with Penny began slowly to pack away the library, her book tin rattled with the few coins she'd received from Mr Gregory earlier in the day as she locked it away in a cupboard.

Fischer recognised the end of the day signals and settled down in the passenger seat to await the journey home.

"Not quite time to go yet, Fish Face," Penny said, settling behind the wheel. She pulled out her book, a bit of fictional nonsense about the life of a celebrity. A rags-to-riches tale that had readers scoffing and cooing in equal measure. Despite herself, Penny was thoroughly swept up in it. She made it a point to read as many types of genre as possible so she was able to recommend them to specific customers. She could devour a few pages of this frothy nonsense now and polish it off later before bed. The pages turned steadily as Penny raced through the easy read, distracted from all her concerns.

As she turned to the end of the chapter, a cliff hanger insisting she read on, she suddenly realised the time. She'd lost track completely while buried in the pages of her book. The library was supposed to have closed a short while ago, and she should be well on her way home by now. Fischer was curled up fast asleep and gently snoring on the seat next to her. She gave him an ear scratch to wake him and with a last minute check for late customers, started the engine.

The small village of Chiddingborne was as picturesque as all the villages of Hampsworthy Downs, and Penny thought herself lucky to have a job that took her around the prettiest parts of the country on a regular basis.

She pulled up at the junction to the main road and looking right for oncoming traffic could see the garden centre in the distance on the opposite side of the road. It was still open on these long, warm summer evenings. She immediately recognised a figure in the car park carrying what looked like a rose tree.

"Look who it is, Fischer," she said to the little dog, who immediately pricked up his ears at the sound of her voice.

Penny changed direction and drove across the road and turned right into the garden centre. Pulling up next to a car she leaned across to wind down Fischer's window.

"Mr Kelly."

"Penny. Hello. And hello to you too, young man," he said to an exuberant Fischer whose tail was wagging furiously at the sight of one of his favourite people.

"I've spotted the red kite twice today," Penny beamed.

"That's excellent news. Do you have time for a pot of tea?"

The tea room inside the garden centre was so full of plants it was like stepping into a jungle. It was lush and green at any time of the year, but summer also brought flashes of colour to the foliage. A parakeet chirped somewhere among the leaves, a clever system of interlocking cages and flight ways let the pair of birds wander through the tea rooms and wider garden centre at will. The male seemed to have chosen to be Mr Kelly's shadow today as the bird remained close by, chattering and whistling away, hidden in the fronds of a thousand plants.

Fischer sat at Penny's feet, cocking his head this way and that as he searched for the owner of the chirping, the little dog hopeful of a new friend to make.

The small wooden garden table had ample room for a pot of tea and the small tower of tiny cakes Mr Kelly had insisted on buying.

"My head teacher pension is more than enough to stretch to a few cakes for my favourite mobile librarian," Mr Kelly said as the waitress departed.

Penny took a small but perfectly formed two tier Victoria sponge the size of a small scone.

"So, tell me about the red kite," Mr Kelly said, pulling out his notebook.

Penny lifted the lid and briefly stirred the tea. "I saw her this morning above Sugar Hill. I was on my way to Rowan Downs, so it must have been just before nine o'clock. She caught something, then flew off in the direction of Cringle Wood. Then I saw her again just after lunch on the way to Chiddingborne."

Mr Kelly jotted down the details in his neat handwriting, picked up the teapot, decorated with a climbing green vine that spiralled around the spout, and poured for the two of them. The steaming amber liquid splashing into two teacups with the same design.

"Terrible news from Rowan Downs," Penny said, feeling her hand shake slightly as she lifted her cup from its saucer.

Mr Kelly was studying his recent notes and looked up immediately at the tone in Penny's voice.

"News? What news?"

"About Mrs Sharp. I'm afraid she was found dead this morning, Mr Kelly."

Mr Kelly looked shocked. "Mrs Sharp? From Chips Ahoy? Oh no, surely you must be mistaken, Penny?"

"I'm afraid not," Penny toyed with her spoon, eyes downcast. "I spoke to Detective Inspector Monroe. He was there himself."

Mr Kelly leaned on the table. The news the detective inspector from Winstoke was in attendance could only mean one thing.

"She died in suspicious circumstances then?" Mr Kelly said heavily.

Penny nodded. "So it would seem."

Mr Kelly picked up his tea and shook his head sadly. Penny could see the slight quiver in his own hand as he took a sip.

"I was in there only last night. Sunday night is always a good night for fish and chips when you don't have the energy to cook a full roast dinner. Have you heard if anyone has been arrested?"

Penny shook her head. "Not as far as I know. It's only just happened. But the death is suspicious or else John Monroe wouldn't have been there. Nor would the crime scene people.

I can't quite bring myself to believe it but everything points to her being murdered."

"Terry Stokes the builder was in there yesterday," Mr Kelly said thoughtfully. "He was shouting at Olive Sharp dreadfully. Such a big man shouting at a little old lady it was horrible to witness. No respect for the elderly nowadays. I had to tell him to calm down and leave.

Penny couldn't help but grin. "You kicked Terry Stokes out of the shop?"

"Well, someone had to. I remember him as a boy, always pushing people around. I had to tell him off more than once as a youngster in the school playground or hallways, I can tell you. Last night was no different. Sadly he doesn't seem to have changed much. He turned on me when I spoke up, but backed down as soon as he realised who it was. The many years I spent teaching small boys means I've perfected my intimidating tone. He's much bigger now than when I taught him, but he's still the same old Terry Stokes. A bully to the core."

Terry Stokes was a local builder and arguably the best one around. He was built like a stack of heavy masonry, a man mountain chiselled from cement blocks. What he lacked in charm and manners he made up for in building skills. It was probably why people tolerated him, Penny thought ruefully.

"Why was he shouting at Mrs Sharp?"

"She'd not yet paid him for a job he'd done for her. A security door or something I think."

Penny took out her notebook and turned to a fresh page. She wrote while Mr Kelly spoke.

"He barged passed the queue and leaned on the counter. Very menacingly I have to say. She didn't budge an inch. I couldn't help but admire her tenacity," Mr Kelly said.

"She was a tough old bird," Penny agreed. "And I don't think anyone could intimidate her, not for money anyway."

"Stokes said he wanted the cash in his account by Monday or he would make her sorry. I don't know what he could have meant by that?"

"There's no doubt Terry Stokes is rough, with a short fuse, but a killer? I know he was told to leave the Pig and Whistle pub in Cherrytree Downs once or twice in his youth for causing trouble, but that was years ago and he's never been known to threaten old ladies as far as I'm aware."

"I was there, Penny, and witnessed him doing just that. He has a bad temper and a short fuse like you say. He blurts out the first thing that comes into his head without engaging his mouth. But after speaking to Mrs Sharp like that I expect John Monroe will want to have a word or two with him."

Penny lifted her cup. Terry Stokes was trouble with a capital T and she wouldn't normally have had anything to do with him. But with no one else available at the time, he'd once mended her fence when it had blown down in a winter storm, and he'd done a brilliant job of it. But he'd complained about the tea she'd made, spitting out the first mouthful and shouting, "What's this rubbish?" Penny had tried to overlook his boorish and vulgar manner, but he made it very difficult for people to like him.

"I know that look, Penny Finch," Mr Kelly said with a chuckle, topping up their tea. "The best known sleuth of Hampsworthy Downs has her investigative hat on I see."

Penny shook her head. "I don't think so, Mr Kelly. Not this time. It has nothing to do with me. I wasn't there. I don't know Terry well, and I never frequented the chip shop. I think I should keep my nose out of this one and leave it to the professionals."

Mr Kelly nodded, eyes sparkling.

"I know that look, too," Penny said. "You don't believe me, do you?"

"The red kite doesn't choose to hunt," Mr Kelly began obscurely. "She circles, riding the thermals. She is content to glide. But when something catches her eye, she feels the hunger and instinct takes over. Then bang. She acts. She has no choice in the matter, it's just in her nature." He finished with a smile and sipped his tea.

Penny laughed. "Well, as beautiful and poetic as that analogy was, I am no bird of prey, Mr Kelly. I am a simple librarian and I hope whatever happened to Mrs Sharp is proved to be no more than a terrible accident. But if there is more to it, then Detective Inspector Monroe is the man for the job. Not me."

As she helped herself to a strawberry tart topped with a dollop of whipped cream, she idly wondered why Terry Stokes would kill Mrs Sharp for a small builder's fee? He was not the most articulate man in the area, but he was far from stupid. A self-employed builder with a reputation for skill as well as temper, he was more than capable of pursuing payment through a small claims court if he was owed money. She doubted it was the first time a customer hadn't paid him. As far as she was concerned, murder was not just a step too far, it was a giant leap of a hundred miles and more. Too far even for someone like Terry Stokes.

"Getting to work on the case, are we, Penny?"

"No," she fibbed with a smile. But even as the denial left her lips, she knew she was already working out her next step.

That evening Penny sat curled up on the sofa with Fischer at her feet. She pulled the woollen blanket over her shoulders as the chill of evening began to creep into her old stone cottage. It was summer and she didn't want to light the wood burner, a blanket, a cup of tea and Fischer was all she needed to keep her warm.

The sun was setting and it was late, nearly ten o'clock, and as she finished the final chapter of her book Fischer suddenly became active. Jumping down from the sofa and dashing to the back door, where he scratched at it impatiently with his paw.

"Want to go out do you, little man?" Penny said, placing her book on a teetering pile next to the sofa. Distracted by Fischer, who'd come running back in, dancing and spinning around the room, she missed her aim and the whole tower tumbled over the floor.

"Oh well, that corner needed a tidy up, anyway." She knelt down and gathered the books and an unfamiliar slim volume among them stood out. It was not one of hers that was for sure. The cover image was of a stylised warrior in ancient armour. This was The Art of War by Sun Tzu, a classic guide to military tactics by an ancient Chinese general. She knew enough about it to answer a few pub quiz questions, but it was not a book she'd studied by any means.

"Edward," she said with a despondent sigh.

Edward Marshall was her former partner. He had left her for a glamorous accountant he'd met through work. Their relationship had been in a holding pattern for years and although she still felt a little betrayed by him for running around behind her back, she also felt a sense of relief that the charade of their relationship was finally over. It wasn't that Edward was a bad man, he was simply not right for her.

She turned the book over and glanced at the sleeve notes. She wondered if he had planned his escape from their relationship with advice from this book; *'When in retreat sound the charge.'* Penny remembered him looking through it one evening when they were having yet another quiet night in. He had informed her it was how he was going to succeed in business, that this book would teach him arcane knowledge which would prove to be as useful in the meeting rooms of a Winstoke accountancy firm as it had been on an ancient Chinese battlefield. Personally Penny had thought that was a load of codswallop, but didn't say so. If Edward really wanted to succeed in his work and life, Penny thought now, he should try the Dale Carnegie classic, *'How to Win Friends and Influence People'* instead. But Edward had always done things his way and she couldn't remember him ever taking advice from her.

Fischer was jumping on her leg, paws scratching and nose snuffling as he tried to get her attention.

"Sorry, Fischer," she said, walking to the door, slapping the Art of War against her thigh. She placed it on the hall table as a reminder to drop it in to Edward's office when she was in Winstoke on Thursday. That was the day she drove to the main library and swapped out the books for a fresh supply.

She looked down at Fischer, patiently waiting for her to let him out. "I just hope he hasn't been defeated in business before I can return his essential guide to success." Fischer barked.

"I know, it's not nice to be sarcastic."

She opened the door and her little dog shot out into the twilight, swiftly doing his business under the old apple tree. He ran back and forth along the back garden wall, sniffing the air. He looked back at Penny briefly, and she was sure he looked disappointed. It was strange, but she could read the little dog's expressions as clearly as she could those of a person. Fischer made another search of the perimeter wall and Penny, standing at the door with a blanket round her shoulders, realised he'd been asking to go out at the same time every night just recently. A few minutes later he hung his head and slunk back to the house. With a final glance over his shoulder, he eventually turned and went back inside.

"What are you looking for, little man? There's nothing there." Penny said, shutting and locking the door. She took him through to the kitchen and gave him a treat, which cheered him up.

What was Fischer looking for? It was almost as if he'd been expecting something to happen, and she couldn't shake the thought. He was an exceptionally clever dog. She peered out of the curtains, but couldn't see anything of interest. She looked down at Fischer and shook her head.

"You're making me jumpy, Fish Face. Come on, let's call it a night."

But he had been expecting something to happen, she was sure of it. There was something on his mind, just like hers. Despite herself, she could not stop thinking about Mrs Sharp.

Three

Tuesday morning and the library pulled into Hambleton Chase. Fischer stood with his paws up on the dashboard, looking out at the world, tail wagging. Penny couldn't imagine her little companion being any happier than she was about work, but it was a close-run thing.

The customers came in a steady stream throughout the morning, never a mad rush, which meant Penny had time to give every patron her attention, but the library was certainly busy enough to justify its costs. Fischer entertained those who were amenable to his repertoire of tricks, from shaking hands to rolling over, all for treats and cuddles, of course. Penny was sure that half the reason the mobile library was so popular was down to her clever little dog.

Toward the end of the morning, Penny saw Mr Edwards. Not a voracious reader by any means, but he had worked his way through her entire collection of pulpy cowboy novels.

Whenever she asked him about the book he'd just read and was returning, he always responded with a dissatisfied and disappointed shrug. She knew he was still looking for that one book that would really excite him.

Mr Edwards was a busy local gardener and was a regular and familiar sight on the roads of Hampsworthy Downs. His green Land Rover and its trailer loaded with gardening machinery and tools was usually parked outside the house where he was working or trundling along the roads between the villages. There was hardly a lawn or a hedge in the area that had escaped the Edwards' treatment. He worked regularly at The Lodge in Holt's End, driving over their huge main lawn on his petrol driven ride-on mower and tending the hedges on the outer boundary of the property.

Some time ago Penny had realised Mr Edwards had never once checked out a gardening book. His knowledge had been acquired over a lifetime of working with his fingers in the soil, undoubtedly aided by a natural talent for all things green.

Today, he looked along the shelves of the little library, paying as much attention to the shelf on needle craft as the action adventure novels. Penny guessed he was here for the company and the visit as much as to get a book. Edwards was never the first to initiate a chat, however Penny had known him long enough to accept that once she started he would talk her ear off. But she had the time.

"Did you hear the terrible news about Mrs Sharp in Rowan Downs?" Penny fully expected the news had already had time to go around the villages by now, but she couldn't be certain if Mr Edwards had heard yet.

"Terrible," he replied, looking at a book on the top shelf, a reference book about the history of powered flight. "Terrible, terrible news." He shook his head and stepped to one side, scanning the new stack of books in front of him. "The best fish and chips I've ever had. But it wasn't just those that were so good. Once when I was working on her garden, just edging the lawn, she brought me a slice of cake and a cup of tea. She wasn't one to give anything away, usually. I nearly dropped my hoe with the shock." Mr Edwards closed his eyes to the memory of that cake. "Best fruit cake I've ever had. Just wonderful. She certainly knew her way around a kitchen. If she had decided to open a fancy restaurant, she would have been full every night. I'm sure she could have given these loud mouth TV chefs a run for their money and they wouldn't have dared use that sort of language in front of her. She was a tough old boot and no mistake. She would have put them in their place in an instant."

Penny nodded, not wanting to interrupt the flow.

"Course, they say Stokes was in there shouting at her. Talk is he went back after dark for his money and killed her."

"Who said that?" Penny asked, automatically reaching for her notebook.

"Oh, everyone," Edwards replied with a wave of his hand and a noncommittal shrug.

Penny knew that whenever someone said 'everyone' it usually meant it was only one or two people actually saying it, but they were saying it to anyone who'd listen and eventually it was repeated ad nauseam. However, it was clear word had spread about Stokes shouting at Mrs Sharp and many were speculating he'd had a hand in her death.

"I don't know if Stokes is guilty of murder," Penny said.

"Oh no, I don't think he did it either," Mr Edwards said, shaking his head and reaching for a cold war thriller. "I've known Stokes a long time. Knew his father, too. Rough as a recently quarried chunk of sandstone, the lot of them. But Terry," Edwards tutted and shook his head again. "He has a nasty temper on him. I've worked alongside him in the past, you know? He was building a wall and I was laying turf at Cherrytree Manor. As cross as a swarm of bees when a honey bear comes along he was, all day. I thought the whole time he would splatter my lawn with cement; he was in such a bad mood he slapped it around all over. But after hours of work there wasn't a single drop anywhere but the wall. And that wall was as neat from one end to the other. A perfect job. But my, oh my, was he miserable. It was all he could do to say hello and goodbye to me, and he did that with nothing more than a grunt."

Penny felt out of breath just listening to Mr Edwards. He slipped the cold war thriller back on the shelf and continued to browse just as her phone vibrated, signalling a text. It was from her friend Susie. She opened the message surreptitiously, not wanting Mr Edwards to think she wasn't giving him her full attention.

'You have to come and meet me asap. I'm in the Pot and Kettle. S x'

Penny slipped her phone away. Whatever Susie wanted, it sounded urgent. Checking the time, she found it was only a few minutes before she was due to pack up for lunch.

"You really liked Murder in Dry Gulch I seem to remember?" Penny said.

Mr Edwards' face lit up. "The cowboy detectives? Yes, that was good. Do you still have it here I'd like to read it again?"

Penny shook her head, thick brown unruly hair dancing. "Unfortunately, I haven't, but this one was returned yesterday. It's about a group of retirees and how they solve a murder. It's got some excellent reviews."

"Just like the retired ranch hands in Murder at Dry Gulch." Edwards picked up the book and turned it over, reading the back cover synopsis. "I'll try it," he said enthusiastically.

Penny shut up shop as Mr Edwards strolled away, already reading the book as he walked along the winding path to his little house. He pulled his nose out of the book just long enough to give her a friendly wave as she drove past, heading out of Hambleton Chase on her way to Thistle Grange to meet Susie at the cafe.

As she got to the outskirts of the village, she slowed down on the lookout for horses and riders crossing the road from the stables, heading out for a gallop in Cringle Wood. The road was clear, but there were fresh signs the horses had recently passed this way. Something Mr Edwards would be pleased to gather up for use around the roses.

Parking safely outside the Pot and Kettle, Penny saw Susie sitting inside at a table. She had a magazine in her hands, a glossy celebrity picture filled monthly stuffed full of cosmetic adverts and quizzes to find out if you were a home maker or a home breaker. She held it up high and was peering over the top of the shiny pages.

Penny clipped on Fischer's lead and jumped out of the van waving at Susie, but her friend was preoccupied and distracted and failed to notice her. What on earth had got her attention?

The bell above the old cafe door tinkled as Penny entered, and a few heads turned to see who it was. Most of them knew Penny, and she waved in response to nods and greetings. Her friend, however, was still hiding behind her magazine.

Fischer tugged on his lead the moment she'd stepped inside and made a beeline for Susie, jumping onto her lap when he was within distance.

Susie jumped in surprise as Fischer fussed over her. She dropped the magazine on the table and looked up, smiling.

"What's happening?" Penny said. Not her usual greeting but she could see from her friend's face something had her attention. She was both amused and conspiratorial. Susie said nothing but patted the chair next to her, inviting Penny to sit.

Penny did so, and Susie once again lifted the magazine, hiding behind it. She pointed into the cafe.

"Don't look," she said in a low voice.

Penny did the one thing everyone does when told not to look at something.

Susie laid a hand on her arm, dragging her attention back and pointed again.

Penny looked in the same direction, more subtlety this time. Susie was pointing at a woman sitting alone at a far corner table. A cup and saucer in front of her along with a partially ripped up serviette, the remains of which were in her hands being twisted and tugged at. Even though she was sitting, Penny could tell the woman was tall and slim. She held herself erect, but there was a slight hunching to her shoulders suggesting to Penny the woman had something worrying on her mind. Her hair was long and wavy, and a beautiful straw coloured blond which looked to be natural. She was strikingly attractive even for a woman who had to be, for all her youthful appearance, late middle age.

Penny turned to Susie, who was grinning and nodding.

"What?" she said, completely at a loss.

"It's her," Susie said. She put the magazine down and scratched Fischer's ears.

"Her who?" Penny asked, genuinely mystified by her friend's strange behaviour.

Susie rolled her eyes. She shook her head in exasperation, then gave Fischer another fuss. He'd been snuffling all around her as though she had dog treats hidden in her pockets.

"Come on, Fischer, time to get down. I know we haven't seen Susie for a week but you'd think we'd not seen her for years the way you're carrying on."

"I know what he wants," Susie said, taking Fischer's little face in her hands and leaning close, "But I'm sorry to disappoint you, Little man, I don't have anything today."

"What do you mean?"

Susie looked at Penny, a bit embarrassed. "I've been feeding him." She admitted.

"Feeding him what? When?"

"Chips."

"Chips?" said Penny in disbelief.

"Well scraps actually, you know the extra batter you always get? I'm not that keen, so I've been giving them to Fischer. Me and the kids have been biking over and getting Fish and Chips from Chips Ahoy almost every night this last week and walking past your garden on the way back. Sorry."

"Oh, Susie. You know I don't agree with giving Fischer *people* food. It's not good for him."

"I know, I know. I am sorry, Penny. Really, I am. It was an accident first time and then he's been waiting each night since."

It then made sense to Penny exactly what Fischer had been looking for the night before.

"It's a long way to go for chips, Susie?"

"I know, but the car's in the garage at the moment and in any case it's something me, Billy and Ellen can do together, they love it."

36

"You should have called in," Penny said, feeling a little disappointed her friend hadn't knocked on the door.

"It's not that we didn't want to," Susie said. "But by the time we reached your house it was always a bit late. Way past the children's bed time, actually. Anyway, we won't be getting chips from anywhere else now. Chips Ahoy was the only place near enough and nothing compares to Mrs Sharp's chips, anyway."

"Do you remember when you thought she'd forgotten to put salt and vinegar on your chips and you asked for more?"

Susie laughed, "Remember? I still have nightmares about it. You'd have thought I'd asked her to hand over the deeds to the shop." Susie gathered herself up to perform an impression. "More salt? Five pence."

Penny grinned. Susie's impression was so good it was almost as if Mrs Sharp was in the room.

"She frightened the life out of me. I could only have been about fourteen or so at the time. I don't think I've dared put extra salt on my chips since."

"She did you a favour," Penny said. "Too much salt isn't good for you."

The pair lapsed into silence, and Susie sighed. "Even though she wasn't the friendliest of people, Mrs Sharp was such a big part of the community. Something all the villages shared. She'll be missed."

"She will. But you didn't bring me here to confess to over feeding Fischer, or to remember Mrs Sharp. So, why are we here, Susie?"

Susie grinned again and pointed, her hand close to the table making short jabbing motions toward the glamorous woman sitting on the other side of the cafe, still worrying her serviette. "I had a tip off that a celebrity was sitting in the Pot and Kettle." Susie said in low tones. "So I grabbed a taxi to get over here to see who it was." She finished with an expectant grin at her friend.

Penny shook her head again. She really had no idea who this person was.

"Coffee," Susie said quietly, half mouthing the word.

"Coffee?" Penny said loudly, and Susie shushed her.

"It's the coffee lady. Remember? The adverts? Dark Roast?" she put on her best impression of a sultry coffee advert voice over. "After dark, a blend of excellence. Dark roast." She grinned and pointed.

Now Penny remembered. The long running string of adverts with the neighbours sharing coffee, and hints of much more after dark. The pair had become a national conversation, an obsession actually. Were the adverts too suggestive? Were the couple ever going to get married? And who drinks coffee after dark anyway? Both actors were instantly recognisable at the time, but it was a long time ago and both had vanished from television screens, never to be seen again.

"And there was that song always playing in the background," Susie said. "Like they both only owned one record, the same record. It was released as a single too, do you remember?"

Penny nodded as snippets of the song slowly came back to her. A soppy romantic ballad. "You remember the song as well?"

"Remember it? I bought it. It was one of my favourites. I could sing it now."

"Please don't. But didn't you like bands with lots of guitars and even more hair?"

Susie shrugged. "What can I say, I had an eclectic taste." Then she grinned as she glanced at the coffee lady again, as excited almost as much as if a member of the royal family had just walked in.

Penny followed her gaze. She'd only ever known her as the coffee woman. She had no name in the adverts and Penny hadn't thought of them in years, not since the last advert had aired. Coffee wasn't really something she found exciting.

Susie held up her phone. She'd already searched the internet and found an actor listing page with her on it. "Chase Scarlett," she said in an excited whisper. "That's her name. What a great name. Sounds very theatrical."

"It is a great name," Penny agreed, trying to match Susie's enthusiasm but failing. "Susie," she said more seriously. "Did you really summon me here just to spy on a former coffee advert actress? From your text I thought it was urgent."

Susie scratched Fischer's head. He'd been curled up on her knee ever since they'd arrived. "I thought you'd be as thrilled as me to have a real celebrity in our midst, Penny. But I might also need a lift back to town." She added, a bit sheepishly. "I was hoping you'd drop me off? I used up the rest of my daily expense allowance on the taxi."

Penny rolled her eyes. "Well, I hope you can get a story out of it. Yes, of course I'll drive you back to town."

No one else in the Pot and Kettle seemed to have noticed a television star among them. Penny saw Chase Scarlett had pulled the serviette entirely to shreds and was oblivious to Susie talking about her. Maybe because she had dealt with being a well-known face a thousand times before and had learned to shut it all out. But as she observed more closely, she could see the woman was in a world of her own.

"What's she doing here?" She wondered out loud.

"Not drinking coffee," Susie said, her girlish enthusiasm doubling her volume. Chase Scarlett heard her then, and Penny noticed a slight twitch in the woman's face. She stood and walked to the counter to pay her bill. She moved like a ghost, silent and graceful, almost drifting over the floor, her red heels hardly making a sound on the cafe's tiled floor.

Susie stood up. "I'm going to say hello."

Penny groaned and took Fischer from her arms, putting him on the floor, and trailed after her friend as she followed the coffee lady outside.

Miss Scarlett?" Susie called out in a friendly tone. "Hello. I'm Susie Hughes. Journalist with the Winstoke Gazette. Do you have a moment? I'm sure my readers would love to know what brings a television celebrity to Hampsworthy Downs."

"It's Ms Scarlett." She replied in a deep voice, rich with a trained actor's quality to it. She slipped on an oversized pair of dark glasses retrieved from a designer handbag.

"Ms Scarlett, of course. Can I ask what brings you here?"

Ms Scarlett stood straight, turning her shoulders, her chin, a foot into a perfect poise. Every move was deliberate and timed to perfection. Although she had not been on television for many years, she was clearly a trained actor through and through.

"No, you may not," she said in well enunciated tones. Then turned and walked away, with Fischer straining at the lead, trying desperately to follow.

Penny and Susie watched her leave.

"Come on," Penny said. "You brought me all this way in my lunch break, the least you can do is share a pot of tea with me."

At that moment a police car drove slowly up the road, PC Bolton at the wheel.

Ms Scarlett stopped in her tracks and did an about turn. She headed back towards Penny and Susie, wafting past them in a miasma of heady scent.

PC Bolton parked his car, and then walked into a nearby garden and around to the back of a house across the road.

"What's he doing out and about?" Susie asked. "It must be serious if he's left his garden."

Then Penny realised it was Terry Stokes' van parked on the drive. A few moments later he appeared with PC Bolton. Bolton looked at Stokes' mud and cement covered overalls, then back at his pristine car.

"Have you got a change of clothes?"

"I'll take my van and meet you there," Terry said.

"Okay, son. Straight to the station now, is that clear? We don't want to keep the inspector waiting."

Terry gave a curt nod.

"They're taking him in for questioning," Susie said. "Maybe I should follow? If they want to talk to him about the chip shop murder, I really should be reporting on it. I might get some information at the police station."

Penny frowned over at the retreating figure of Chase Scarlett. "What about our visiting celebrity?"

Susie looked from Terry to Chase and back again, unable to make up her mind.

"Come on," Penny said. "Mrs Sharp is more important to the people who read your paper than an old TV advert. Let's go."

Penny climbed into the mobile library's driving seat and found it unbearably hot from sitting in the sun. She wound down the windows while Susie settled in the passenger seat with a happy little dog on her knee.

"Right, let's go and see what this is all about. I won't be able to stay long though as need to get the library back to Hambleton Chase for the afternoon."

Four

The police station in Winstoke was a beautiful Victorian building erected using huge yellow sandstone blocks interspersed with red brick. Large original white framed sash windows had withstood the battering of hundreds of winter storms and thousands of days under the brilliant warmth of a summer's midday sun. The station was on the side of a busy street running through the centre of town, merging with the roads that led away to the village of Rowan Downs and up through the market centre to the farmland and hills beyond.

Although Penny was used to town, it seemed much busier than usual. She pulled up at the side of the road and parked the library behind Terry's van and PC Bolton's car. Susie was out and chasing the police officer as he escorted Terry Stokes up the steps before she'd pulled on the handbrake. She grabbed Fischer's lead and, after locking up, followed her friend.

"Are you under arrest, Mr Stokes?" Susie called out as the man was led inside.

He turned angrily. "Keep your nose out of it, Hughes," he spat angrily.

PC Bolton made sure Stokes was inside the building before he turned, heading back down the steps. He looked at Susie, puffing himself up, ready to field any questions from the press. Susie ignored him and called out to Stokes again.

"Do you want to give your side of the story to the paper, Terry?"

"You might as well get off, Susie Hughes. There's nothing for you here." PC Bolton said with an air of importance.

"Why, have you eaten all the biscuits again?" she muttered under her breath.

"I heard that." Bolton replied.

Penny grabbed Susie's elbow and dragged her past Bolton up the steps towards the door.

"And what do you want? Someone not paid their book fine?" Bolton chuckled and waddled back to his car, annoyed he hadn't got a rise from Penny, who was taking no notice of him.

The tiled waiting area inside the old building was cool and a relief from the heat outside. Penny's trainers squeaked as she walked over the polished floor. Terry Stokes was sitting on the wooden bench next to the hatch where the station duty officer could speak to members of the public. The sliding panel was shut, frosted glass blocking the view of the office beyond.

The waiting bench had to be as old as the building itself and looked more like a church pew. The timber was solid and smooth with the patina of age and countless rears polishing it to a near mirror shine. Not even the vast bulk of Terry Stokes could challenge it. Stokes narrowed his eyes when Penny and Susie walked in, then stretched his arms over the back support taking up as much space as possible so they couldn't sit down.

Luckily, John Monroe chose that moment to enter the room from a side door which separated the back office from the public area. A young detective sergeant in a smart suit and loose tie just behind him.

Monroe faltered for a second upon seeing Penny, then turned to Terry.

"Thank you for coming in, Mr Stokes. Go with the detective here and I'll be with you in a moment."

Stokes stood up, towering menacingly over the young detective, who to his credit didn't flinch one bit.

"John, hello," Penny said once Stokes had gone. She realised she had no reason to be here and felt suddenly uncomfortable.

"Penny," he said brightly, but with a hint of concern in his voice. "What brings you here? Is everything all right?"

"Is Terry Stokes under arrest?" she blurted out, then wished she hadn't. Monroe stiffened slightly, and she felt his attitude toward her change.

"This is a police matter, Penny. I can't discuss it with you."

"Is he under arrest, Detective Inspector?" Susie repeated in her official reporter voice, stepping forward, notebook and pen in hand.

"Ah, Mrs Hughes, I didn't see you there. Mr Stokes is helping us with our enquiries." He turned back to Penny.

"You must know I can't give out any information to you and certainly not to the press."

"Is it because of the altercation between Terry and Mrs Sharp at the chip shop the night she was murdered?" Penny asked.

"In part," Monroe sighed, and Penny watched him weigh up how much he could tell them against the rumours currently circulating. "We've had information from an eye witness who said he'd seen a man leaving the rear of Chips Ahoy late on Sunday evening."

"Who is your informant, Inspector?" Susie asked as scribbled notes.

Monroe almost laughed. "Not an informant, Mrs Hughes. This isn't some spy drama. A concerned member of the public reported it."

"Anyone I know?" Penny said. She knew most people in the area. It was a small community with the mobile library right at the heart of it.

Before he could answer, the door to the offices opened and a short, scruffy man with blond unwashed and unbrushed hair stepped out. He smiled up at Monroe.

"Thanks for the tea, John," with a familiarity that bordered on insolence. "Anything else you need to know about what I saw, just call in. I've no phone but you know where to find me."

Penny recognised the man, he was somewhat of a local celebrity. He'd lived around the villages and hamlets of Hampsworthy Downs for years. Some said he was a tramp, others an eccentric millionaire. Although Penny couldn't understand, if the latter was true, why someone with money would choose to wear such tatty clothes and hardly ever wash. He would surely at least by himself a decent pair of shoes.

Fischer hid behind Penny, lead wrapped around her legs, and stayed out of reach until the scruffy man had left the building.

"Eddie Tompkins?" Penny said. "That's where you got your information?"

Monroe looked a little flustered and more than a little embarrassed to have been found out. Penny knew he could deny Tompkins was the informant, but it was obvious from the brief exchange she'd just witnessed that Eddie Tompkins had just dropped Terry Stokes in it.

"Penny, I can't talk at the moment. Mr Stokes has kindly come in to answer a few questions. We have to follow up all lines of enquiry. Unless you have anything important for me I must press on."

"So, should I take it that you do not have a prime suspect at this moment, Inspector Monroe?" Susie asked while she scribbled. "Should the residents of Hampsworthy Downs be concerned there is a murderer on the prowl?"

"Mrs Hughes, I know it's your job, but could you please try not to be so melodramatic? We understand the distress this death has caused, and we'd like to reassure the public we are doing everything in our power to bring this case to a swift resolution. My team and I are working around the clock to make sure Hampsworthy Downs and the local area continues to be a safe place for residents and visitors alike. There," he said. "A brief statement for your readers."

Monroe stepped closer to Penny, friendly as he held an arm out around her, but stopped just short of actual contact. Penny could see his jacket was clean and sharp, his tie in a perfectly executed Windsor knot, his hair neatly brushed and smelling faintly of aftershave, a pleasant scent, masculine but not overpowering.

"Can I have a quick word, Penny?" Then to Susie, "Excuse us one moment, Mrs Hughes."

Penny let him guide her to a far corner of the public area.

"Penny," he started with a kind but authoritative tone. "It's not that I don't admire your ability to sniff out a clue but please, this is a police matter and if it is proved to be murder, then it's probably wise to let me and my team handle the investigation. If there is a murderer on the loose, and I'll stress again, *if*, then I don't want you anywhere near... them."

"You were going to say him, weren't you?" Penny said.

Monroe smiled but didn't answer. "As a friend, please, will you leave this investigation alone?"

"I don't want to get involved. I am more than happy to drive around in my library and talk to people about books. The only reason I am here is because Susie needed a lift. She's the one asking the questions."

Monroe looked at Penny with a half smile. "I have built my career on listening out for lies and the reasons people tell them. If you are not lying to me, then you are lying to yourself. You're a natural detective, Penny Finch, and interested in listening to people. It's how detectives work. People can't help but talk and invariably the truth comes out whether they intend it to or not. Please, excuse the clichés, but I can see you're drawn to this investigation like a moth to a flame. I just don't want to see you get burned, that's all."

Penny knew in heart John Monroe was right. She was drawn to the case and wanted to get to the truth of what happened to Mrs Sharp as much as anyone. She also thought eventually, somehow, she could get it.

"Promise me you'll stay away from the investigation, Penny? I really am concerned for your safety."

Penny smiled at him, but couldn't find it in herself to make a promise she might not be able to keep.

Monroe sighed and held her gaze for a second before bending down and scratching Fisher's ears. He delivered a final goodbye to them all and made his way back to the rear offices.

Penny's heart was pounding.

Susie grinned at Penny. "What did he say?"

Penny led them out of the station and across to the grassed area opposite for Fischer, and waited for him in the brilliant sunshine before replying. "He asked me to leave the investigation alone and not get involved."

"Right. So nothing about how nice you look or how shiny your hair is, or how attractive you look in those scruffy trainers?"

"Susie, this is not middle school."

"I know that, Miss Completely Clueless, but anyone can see he likes you."

"I think he's just concerned I'll mess up the investigation if I start snooping."

Susie shrugged. "It's a pity I didn't get to talk to Ms Scarlett, but maybe I have a bigger story here." She waved her notebook.

"I really need to be on my way, Susie, I'll have customers wondering where I am if I don't get my skates on. Do you need a lift back to work?" Penny dug in her bag for her van keys.

"No, don't worry, I can walk from here. Thanks for the lift."

"Anytime," Penny replied, and meant it. Susie was her best friend, and it was no trouble to help her out.

Susie headed off to the newspaper offices, flicking through her notebook as she walked. Penny opened the camper van and let Fischer jump in and get settled before she climbed aboard.

"Okay, Fischer, let's get back to work."

As she drove out of Winstoke, she saw Eddie Tompkins walking along the side of the road. She guessed he was heading back to his caravan. It crossed her mind to give him a lift, it would hardly be out of her way but one look at the dashboard clock and she found she really didn't have time. Besides, he walked everywhere and it was a beautiful day. He'd probably decline her offer anyway. He wasn't really a people person. And glancing at her little furry companion, she remembered his reaction when Eddie had come into the police station waiting area. That clinched it. She didn't want Fischer upset.

Pulling into her spot in Hambleton Chase with scarcely a minute to spare, Penny saw several customers milling about waiting for her, and numerous others walking her way. She jumped down and let Fischer out, then opened the side doors. The library was open for business. As her first customers climbed into the back of the van to peruse the book selection, Penny dug out her camping stove and a pack of sandwiches. All that running around at lunchtime and she hadn't even stopped for a cup of tea or some food. There hadn't been time at the Pot and Kettle. She filled Fischer's water bowl and gave him a handful of biscuits, then settled down in her deckchair. Even on a day as warm as this, there was nothing quite as refreshing as a nice cup of tea.

Penny was kept busy all afternoon and when the last of the library users left, she thought it was a real shame to have to pack up for the day. It was lovely sitting and relaxing here. She was in no hurry to leave until she received a call.

"Hi, it's me."

"Hi, Susie, I'm just packing up for the day."

"Me too. Can you give me a lift back?"

"Home? Yes, of course. I can be in Winstoke in about twenty minutes."

"Maybe we could make a quick stop on the way back?"

"Yes, okay. Where do you need to go?" She asked, shutting the van doors now she'd finished packing up.

"You know where Eddie Tompkins' caravan is, don't you? I need to talk to him."

Penny hesitated. She didn't particularly want to stop by Tompkins' caravan. Aside from the fact she didn't like the man much, she felt as though she was betraying Monroe slightly by taking Susie for a friendly chat after he had asked her, politely but quite firmly, to leave the investigation alone. But Penny could hardly let her friend go by herself. And she knew Susie well enough to know she'd find some way to get there with or without Penny. The very idea of leaving Susie unaccompanied in the middle of a field with that man gave her the chills. There was just something about him that made her cringe. Nothing she could put her finger on, it was just she didn't trust him.

"All right, I'll be there soon."

Eddie Tompkins' caravan was in a field on the side of the main road from Rowan Downs to Winstoke. As the only road from the main town to the six villages and hamlets that made up Hampsworthy Downs, Penny passed this way every time she went to the main library or Winstoke town for other reasons. The tall hedgerows hid his makeshift home from sight, and she'd never given it much thought until now.

Susie had been waiting at the junction when Penny had approached the outskirts of town and now sat peering through the camper van windscreen, leaning further forward the nearer they got. Finally, a few minutes away from Rowan Downs,

Penny parked in a small lay-by next to the old farm five-bar gate, backed with chicken wire, which had almost been swallowed by the unchecked hedgerow. Taking it in turns to hold Fischer, they climbed over and walked along the beaten earth path that fringed the overgrown field. Fischer trotting happily alongside them, sniffing out new tantalising scents.

Eddie Tompkins' caravan was a weather beaten old 1970s model. It had once been the pride and joy of a family and had no doubt seen many a happy holiday in the British seaside towns up and down the country. Now in its retirement it sat alone in the corner of a field, green from weather stains and lichen, partly overgrown with brambles and missing a tyre from one of its rusty wheels. It would never trundle along the country roads again.

Susie stopped a few feet from the battered door, Penny sure that if they knocked the whole door would cave in. Possibly taking the entire caravan with it. No matter how unkempt and derelict it looked, it was still someone's home and Penny didn't want to be the one to demolish it.

"Eddie," Susie called out. She took another step forward. "Eddie, are you there? It's Susie Hughes from the paper. I was hoping to have a quick chat?"

The brown and orange circle patterned curtain at the window, a relic from the sixties, twitched slightly. Somewhere in the dark recesses of the battered vehicle, someone was watching. Then a voice called out.

"Is that Penny Finch from the library with you?"

"Yes, Eddie, it is. Fischer too, he's friendly."

"I'm not paying that fine," Eddie shouted.

Penny furrowed her brow for a moment, then remembered some years ago Eddie had borrowed a book on meditation and brought it back several months late. The fine, while the biggest she could remember issuing, was hardly more than the price of a cup of tea. He'd not been back to the library since, but at least he had returned the book.

"That was a long time ago, Eddie," Penny said. "I don't think anyone remembers it." Except her, she thought. Because she'd been the one to pay the fine from her own pocket.

"What do you want? I'm busy."

"I just want to ask you a few questions about Mrs Sharp," Susie said, taking another step forward.

Penny watched the green algae tinted window, held in place by clumps of bright green moss and something else brown and unidentifiable, for signs of movement. Fischer sat at her heel, quiet and still except for the twitching of his nose as he sniffed the air. She saw a line strung from one end of the caravan and tied off in the hedge. It was hung with rabbit skins and Penny's stomach gave a lurch, and she felt the bile rise in her throat.

The caravan door burst open suddenly, a cloud of steam spewing forth and Eddie dropped to the ground, a short scarred and blood stained club hung on the back of the door. Behind Eddie in the gloom, Penny could see steam rising from a large pot on the stove, a flame licking around its blackened bottom. Penny stepped back, repulsed by the smell. It didn't take a genius to work out what was being boiled.

Eddie smirked as he watched her retreat, assuming she was offended by him. He loved to repulse people, especially those who encroached on his privacy.

Fischer stayed quiet and still at Penny's side, but watched Eddie's every move with intelligent and wary eyes.

"I paid the fine for you, Mr Tompkins," Penny said brightly. "We're not here about that. We wanted to ask if you knew anything about what happened to Mrs Sharp."

"You know I do. That's why I was at the police station. I saw you both there," he growled at her. "I saw someone leaving there that night."

"Was it Terry Stokes?" Susie asked.

"Probably. I don't care. Everyone knows he's a thug and a bully. I wouldn't put it past him to do old Sharp in. It was dark so I couldn't be sure who it was, but they were tall, like Stokes, so it was probably him that killed her. I was glad I told the police what I saw."

"Did you tell the police it was actually Stokes you saw?" Susie flipped open her note book.

"What I said to the police, Missy, is between them and me. But they can throw Stokes in jail for murder for all I care. Whether he did it or not."

"Could it have been someone else?"

Tompkins stared into the distance, his mind elsewhere.

"Why were you there, Eddie?" Penny asked. "What were you doing round the back of the chip shop at midnight?"

Tompkins glared at her. "I never said midnight. You trying to trip me up or something?"

Penny sighed inwardly. Her little gambit hadn't paid off. She should have realised it would fail. For all his outward appearance, Eddie Tompkins was a very intelligent man in a devious and sly sort of way. He wouldn't be fooled so easily. She'd plucked the time out of thin air. An educated guess based on the fact Mrs Sharp usually shut the shop at about eleven on a Sunday night, and she'd spend an hour or so cleaning before she locked up. Whoever killed her would need to do it after she'd closed.

"So, why were you there?"

"None of your business," he replied, giving her a mean look.

"No, you're right," Penny said, backing down. "We apologise, Mr Tompkins, we shouldn't have bothered you." She turned to walk away.

Susie sidled up to her and spoke in a harsh whisper. "Penny, don't go. He knows something."

And Penny knew something, too. She knew Tompkins wanted to talk to them, wanted them to know how clever he was. Penny noticed more about Eddie Tompkins than he would have liked. She recognised he was intelligent but also, despite his appearance and his strange manner, he was vain. He liked to draw attention to himself. If he didn't, he would dress in clean clothes, wash himself and comb his hair. He would wear shoes in the summer rather than walk about barefoot. No, it was all for the shock value. He wanted people to talk and wonder about him, she'd noticed that the few times he'd visited the library. He always picked the strangest, most obscure and controversial title he could find, then raise his voice so others could hear what he'd chosen. No, there was nothing so different about Eddie Tompkins apart from an exaggerated need to appear different. She was banking on his need to gloat and for an audience when she turned away. Her gambit paid off.

"I was there because Mrs Sharp gave me chips. Every night. Leftover chips and sometimes a bit of fish or a sausage. People said she was mean, but she was always kind and generous to me. She was an outsider too, see."

"She fed you?" Penny asked in surprise, turning back to face him.

"Every night after closing she'd put something out for me, well wrapped. I'd wait out of sight then collect them after she'd gone."

"So you were there when someone went in the back door?" Susie asked.

"No, I didn't see anyone enter, I only saw them leave. The back door was open and I was waiting out of sight when they came out. It must have been Stokes, and he killed her because she owed him a bit of money for a door. I hope they throw away the key. Where am I going to get my chips now?"

The sound of a saucepan lid rattling on a boiling pan and the hiss of water hitting a hot plate came from the caravan. A fresh blast of boiling meat wafted into the night air, and Penny covered her nose and turned away from the stench, gagging.

"Now, get off my land," Eddie said and returned inside, slamming the door.

Penny gave Fischer's lead a gentle tug, and he trotted alongside her. Susie followed on the narrow path, making their return journey.

"Is it really his land?" Susie asked as they approached the wooden gate.

"I don't know, but it should be easy enough to find out," Penny said, handing Fischer to Susie while she climbed over the gate.

With them both settled back in the van with Fischer on Susie's knee, Penny turned to her friend and said, "I don't know if we can trust anything Eddie Tompkins says."

"Do you think he did it? Did he actually kill Mrs Sharp and now he's trying to shift the blame onto Terry Stokes?"

"I really don't know," Penny said as she started the engine. "If that was the case, you'd think the last place he would want to be was the police station, unless he enjoyed taunting them, trying to set the blame on someone else when it was him all along. It's the sort of game I can see him playing actually, he's clever enough."

"I don't like him." Susie said with a shudder.

Penny checked her mirrors, flicked on the indicator, then pulled out onto the deserted road. "I don't like him either, Susie, but that doesn't mean he's a killer."

Penny drove back to Cherrytree Downs and dropped Susie off outside her house before heading home. She was desperate for a shower and a change of clothes. She could feel and smell the residue after standing in the steam from Eddie's boiling pot, and it was making her queasy. Once she was fresh and clean, with her clothes shoved into the laundry basket, she headed over to see her parents. She'd had a long and busy day, and a relaxing time with her mum and dad was exactly what she needed.

Fischer pulled frantically as they walked. It was a familiar route through the village, and he knew exactly where they were going. It was early evening but still warm and the path was radiating the day's heat, so Penny moved to the grass verge so Fischer's paws weren't hurt. In the distance Penny could hear the sounds of the countryside; tractors in the fields, the soft hum of bees and the birds tweeting in the trees.

Her mother pulled open the door as Penny opened the gate.

"I thought that was you, love. Come in and I'll pop the kettle on." Her mother gave her a peck on the cheek, then patted her knees. "Come on, Fischer, let's go and learn some new tricks. I've been getting some ideas from You Tube."

Penny laughed. "Oh no, mum, what have you got planned now?"

"Let's just say you will be able to go on one of those talent shows before much longer."

Penny unclipped Fischer's lead, and he raced into the kitchen, sitting next to the cupboard where his treats were kept.

The front room was bright with evening sunshine, the window open, letting in the light breeze scented with honeysuckle and roses. Her father, Albert Finch, was sitting in his chair reading the paper when she entered, a cup of tea and a Garibaldi biscuit on a table by his side.

Penny gave him a kiss on the top of his head and looked at the paper over his shoulder. He was reading Susie's article about the proposed new development of commuter flats in the area.

"Hi, dad."

"Hello, love. Had a good day?"

"Busy, but yes, it's been fine. How about you?"

"There's a lot to be said for retirement in this weather. I've been pottering about in the garden, mostly. Shame about these flats, isn't it? No one wants them here. If it wasn't for Susie's reports none of us would have known a thing about it." He tapped the article in frustration. "We cannot let them tear into the villages like this, Penny."

The flats had been a talking point for some time. A property developer wanted to build a set of American style luxury condominiums. A walled garden community containing small but high-end apartments with a central courtyard which would either be gardens or possibly an outdoor swimming pool. It was aimed at city professionals who were looking for commuter homes. The advantages were numerous. The train station was relatively near and could take workers from the heart of the city to the countryside in a very short time, and the costs of the residences far cheaper to both buy and run compared to those in the capital where the price per square foot was through the roof. Not to mention the health benefits of living in a clean air environment.

"I thought that development had been cancelled?" Penny said. "But I suppose these people will never stop. I can see their point though, who wouldn't want to live in such a beautiful place."

"True, Penny, but if they close themselves off behind gates and walls then they aren't really living here, are they?" Albert said. "A village is more than houses and fields and independent shops. It is a community. You should understand that with the job you have."

"I do, dad. I see how important the community is every day. But Cherrytree Downs is too far out of the way for the commuter crowd. Surely we won't have any development here?"

"But Rowan Downs isn't too far away from us, Penny, just a couple of miles. And if they start nibbling away at the edge of one of the villages, it will most certainly start encroaching on ours too. Then before long these six villages will all be one town to rival Winstoke. And now that poor Olive Sharp has passed away, with her shop in a prime development location, there might not be anybody to stop them going ahead this time. It was only her obstinate refusal to sell the shop that prevented it from happening last time. Unless someone can outbid the developers and reopen the shop, I fear it will go ahead. There was precious little happiness in that home. Pulling it down and building fancy apartments would mean just more unhappiness for Rowan Downs. It will lose everything that makes that village a community."

Mr and Mrs Sharp were blessed with only one child, a son who had died tragically. A well known and well-liked young man, he'd been charismatic like his father and steadfast like his mother. Joining the navy, he'd died while on active duty when a freak weather event had struck during a training exercise taking the lives of all those on board. It was that event above all others that had changed Olive Sharp beyond all recognition. They'd moved to the area from the South West when Penny had been a child, and even after years of living in the area, Mrs Sharp had retained a hint of her original accent.

"Do they have any family who'd want the business?" Penny asked her father, sipping the tea her mother had just brought in.

"Not that I know of. As far as I recall, it was just those two. Must have been a bit lonely for them now I think about it. More so for Olive all these years after losing her husband."

"No one is ever truly lonely in Rowan Downs, dad."

Albert peered over his glasses and gave Penny a smile. "You are a very special young woman, Penny Finch. You make me and your mother very proud even though we don't say it often enough."

She got up to give her dad a hug. He was, like a lot of men of his generation, not overly tactile, but he showed his love and affection in many other ways. He happily received a hug, patting her back in response. The living room door opened and Sheila Finch walked in with Fischer jumping on his back legs, trying to reach the treat in her hand. She dropped it and the little dog caught it as it fell.

"Watch this, you two." She gained Fischer's attention with another treat. Then at her command he weaved in and out of her legs, running a figure eight. Penny stood with her hand on her dad's shoulder, smiling as her mother and Fischer entertained them with his new tricks.

Fischer smiled as he performed, jumping excitedly to collect his reward. The fun was infectious.

"Mum, that was brilliant. Fischer, you are such a clever boy!"

"Shall I get the application for the talent show filled in then, Penny?"

"Not for me, mum, but if you and Fischer want to audition, then feel free." She said, laughing.

No matter what sort of day she had, Penny always knew a visit to her parents could lift her mood.

They stayed for a further hour before Penny decided it was time to go home. On the way out of the door, her mother reminded her they would be away on Saturday morning. As members of the National Trust, they were visiting one of the stately homes in the area for the day then having dinner out.

"Have fun," Penny said as she waved goodbye at the gate and set off for her cottage.

Five

Back at home Penny was settling in for the night when Fischer ran to the back door, scratching to be let out. She opened it and watched him run around for a while, sniffing and staring intently at the gate.

"Oh, Fish Face, I'm sorry, but Susie and the children aren't coming. Come on, time for bed."

But at the slightest sound from outside, the little dog was scratching at the door, tail wagging and looking hopeful.

"It's not her," Penny said for the umpteenth time. "Just someone walking home from the pub, I expect. Susie's at home in bed, exactly where I would like to be. There won't be any more fish and chip scraps for you I'm afraid, little man."

Fischer was addicted to the crispy treat. There must have been some secret ingredient in Mrs Sharp's batter that he couldn't get enough of. The same thing that made people come from miles around just to buy them. Well, whatever it was, she'd never know now. Mrs Sharp had taken it to the grave with her.

Penny curled up in bed, but with Fischer busy downstairs worrying at the back door she couldn't get to sleep for ages. When she finally woke with the sun streaming in through the window, she felt as though she'd hardly had more than five minutes all night.

Wednesday was a busy day in her week. Penny dragged herself out of bed, thick headed and sleepy eyed and got ready on auto-pilot in a sleep-deprived daze. She took a travel mug from the back of the cupboard with the intention of filling it with strong black tea, an imported blend she kept on hand for such mornings, but instead grabbed the wrong box and filled it with her new Fennel blend.

"Oh, good grief. Let's start again."

Reaching for the black tea, she dislodged the box of Fennel and much to Fischer's delight it spilled to floor. Fischer went nuts, lapping it up in an excited frenzy.

"No, Fischer, that tea isn't for you," Penny said, dragging him away and getting a floor cloth from under the sink. She had to clean one handed while holding Fischer back, his determination to get to the tea so strong.

"Now I must make my proper tea and get on otherwise we'll be late."

After Fischer had spent half an hour in the garden, she bundled him into the van and they set off.

Fischer seemingly had no ill effects from his restless night. He sat in his seat watching the world go by as eagerly as he always did, smiling and letting out a soft huff if he spotted a bird or a cow.

"I wish I had half as much energy as you do, Fish Face," Penny said, reaching across and ruffling his ears.

The morning library session in Holts End was as pleasant as ever. Talking to the customers about their book selections was just the pick-me-up Penny needed, and she was slowly brought back to life with all the activity. It was a misty morning to start with, but it was soon burned away with the heat of the sun. Fischer lay snoozing under the van, getting up to greet his favourite customers and to be made a fuss of, then retreating back into the cool of the shade.

During quieter moments, Penny grabbed a random book and sat in her deck chair to read. She'd read twenty pages or more before realising it was one she'd already read, but decided to carry on, anyway. She couldn't recall how it ended but knew one of the characters had a secret life which was about to be revealed, and was swept along for the second time. The only thing better than reading a new book was reading one you had previously enjoyed but had forgotten all about.

With the morning session almost at an end and the last of her regulars supplied with fresh bundles of books for the week ahead, Penny began to pack up. She was almost finished when she was disturbed by her phone vibrating in her pocket.

"You will not believe what I've just found out," Susie's voice exclaimed excitedly.

"Go on, what is it?" Penny said, closing the van doors one handed while juggling the phone in the other.

"Chase Scarlett's real name is Beryl Sharp."

Penny climbed into the driving seat with Fischer clambering up beside her, where he proceeded to curl up and promptly fall asleep on the warm front seat.

"Lots of actors change their name. And let's face it, Susie, Chase Scarlett is much more glamorous than Beryl Sharp so it's hardly surprising she did away with it."

"Sharp," Susie said pointedly. "She's Mr Sharp's sister. Olive Sharp's sister-in-law."

Penny, in her tired state, took a moment to process what her friend was telling her. Could it be a coincidence that Mrs Sharp died on the same day her sister-in-law had turned up?

"Yes, okay, I'll admit that's strange. Sorry, I didn't sleep well and I'm not firing on all cylinders this morning. I wonder if John Monroe knows?"

"I've done a bit of digging and found out she's staying at Thatchings. Can you give me a lift over there?"

"Of course I will," Penny said. "How long will your car be in the garage, Susie?"

"One more day. Last lift, I promise."

"I'm happy to help you know that. I'm due in Thistle Grange this afternoon, and as Thatchings is in Hambleton Chase, it's on the way."

Susie thanked Penny profusely before she hung up.

Fischer was still sound asleep when Penny started the engine and she was just thinking she could easily curl up and have a snooze too, when he stretched and sat up. Resuming his usual position; watching the world go by as Penny drove to pick up Susie.

On the drive back to Hambleton Chase, Susie told Penny everything she'd found out about Chase Scarlett. Penny couldn't concentrate on the road and listen to Susie, so she was glad when they finally arrived at the bed and breakfast. Gary Tait was unloading supplies from the back of his worn out hatchback car when she pulled up and parked.

Thatchings had been run by the senior Taits until their retirement at the end of the last summer. They still lived in a small bungalow at the back of the B&B, but the business was now run by their son, Gary Tait and his wife, Cheryl. Gary was friendly but quiet and more than a little shy. Cheryl, by contrast, was not shy in the slightest and nowhere near as friendly. She had a severe look with straight shoulder-length blond hair, which she cut herself as it was economical. She was notoriously cautious with money. Some admired her thriftiness, others thought her just plain mean.

"If you're looking for a room you're in luck," Gary said, grabbing a couple of boxes from the boot. "We have someone just checking out now so if you can wait for an hour I'll have it ready for you then. You can use the sitting room and gardens while you wait."

"I'm not a guest," Penny said. "It's me, Penny Finch. Don't you recognise me, Gary?"

Gary squinted at her and pulled out his glasses from his top shirt pocket. Sliding them on as he peered in her direction.

"Penny," he said brightly.

Gary had always been very sweet on her and she sensed he'd really wanted to be more than friends, but Penny could never see him in any other way. He was kind and gentle, and his parents were a friendly local couple. By the time she returned from university, Gary had already married Cheryl.

"Hello, Gary, I haven't seen you for a while. You've not changed a bit."

And it was true. He was just as slim and pale as he'd always been. Thin hair neatly combed to one side, thick glasses perched on his nose.

"Hi there, Gary," Susie said, stepping forward. "I'm hoping to have a chance to speak with Chase Scarlett."

"Oh. Hello, Susie. Cheryl is just calling her a taxi now."

"Right. Mind if we come in?"

Gary nodded and indicated Penny and Susie should follow. Fischer trotted alongside Penny, tail wagging with the expectancy of visiting somewhere new, as she followed Susie through the door.

The low roof had thick thatch that came down over the top of the door frame, and Penny had to duck slightly as she stepped inside. The ancient stone walls were painted white in an effort to lighten the interior, but the tiny windows with their original lead breaking them up into small squares, and the low dark oak roof beams meant the inside was still quite dark.

Every effort had been made to bring a sense of warmth and comfort into the place, with chintz covered furniture and standard lamps with velvet shades and brasses hung on the inglenook fireplace. It must be lovely on a cold winter's evening, Penny thought. Thatchings was among the oldest buildings in the area, and she could imagine in years gone by the King's men cantering up on horses demanding a roof for the night and a tankard of ale from busty wenches.

Chase Scarlett was standing at the reception desk, a dark solid piece of timber that was so heavily polished it gleamed. Cheryl Tait was taking a credit card payment. Her lank hair and thin lips devoid of colour were in stark contrast to the rich coloured surroundings. Her lips disappeared as she noticed the newcomers.

"Susie Hughes and Penny Finch." She said it like a curse. "What can I do for the two of you?"

"We were hoping to have a quick word with your guest," Penny said with a smile. It was not returned.

Penny stepped forward. "Ms Scarlett, we just wanted to ask you about Olive Sharp?"

Chase Scarlett turned round sharply. She was tall and her head almost touched the low beam.

"Get out, Penny," Cheryl said in a shrill tone, wagging a finger at her and pointing to the door. "I don't want you here harassing my guests."

Ms Scarlett took her payment card from Cheryl and slipped it back in her purse. Penny could see her hands were shaking.

"Gary will carry your bags," Cheryl said, as he walked in carrying further boxes of supplies. "When you've finished messing about with those boxes, you can carry Ms Scarlett's bags, Gary. And escort these two out," she added with a wave of her hand.

Penny had hardly ever spoken a word to Cheryl, but the woman had obviously formed an unfavourable opinion of her. Gary hurriedly placed the boxes on a side table then scurried over to pick up the bags as ordered to by his wife.

"You are Mrs Sharp's sister-in-law, aren't you, Ms Scarlett?" Susie said. "Did you visit her at all during your stay here?"

Scarlett turned to face Susie, wiping her cheek with a slim hand. "Yes, I visited her. It's the reason I came to Hampsworthy Downs."

"Why are you leaving?" Penny asked.

Chase stopped in her tracks. She looked at Penny, and her lips began to quiver. "It was me. I did it," she cried, her forearm across her brow. "I can't take it anymore. I confess. It was me." She strode to a large armchair and flung herself into it, hands covering her face as she bawled. Huge, pitiful, and convulsing sobs that wracked her slim frame.

Penny and Susie stared at one another in shock.

"I killed her," Chase continued, looking at the stunned audience surrounding her. "I went to see her. My brother bought the shop with money I had given him, money I earned from my career in television. He always told me it was only a loan. I wanted my share of the business to invest in a theatre project, a sure-fire hit, but Olive wouldn't return my calls or answer my letters, so I was forced to travel here to try to make her see reason. I went to the shop just after closing on Sunday night. She was putting out a wrapped package when I arrived so I followed her in, it was dark."

She shifted position in the chair, clasping her hands together against her breast as though in prayer. She turned her head and tilted her chin, thick dark lashes fluttering over water filled eyes as the sun streamed through the small window, turning tears into glowing gems as they slowly travelled down her cheek. Penny nearly glanced behind her, waiting for the director to shout 'cut, that's a wrap.'

"She always hated me," Chase continued. "My glamorous lifestyle. We argued." Scarlett looked up and bit her lip. "She refused to give me any share of the money to fund my play. The script is a work of genius by a clever young writer and my co-star is a veteran of stage and screen. A household name. We were set to light up theatres the length and breadth of the country. I tried to persuade her but she wouldn't hear of it. In frustration, I grabbed her arms. She slipped on the floor, fell backwards, and banged her head on the table. A large vat of batter fell with her. There was batter everywhere and blood. Batter and blood. It was horrifying. I panicked."

Suddenly she threw her arms and head on the arm of the chair, back heaving up and down as she once more broke into sobs. "I was afraid, and I ran. I came here to my hotel but found fear had gripped me and I couldn't move."

She glanced up at the four onlookers. "And now just as I try to leave," once again the back of her hand flew to her forehead, "I am discovered. My terrible, brutal crime is revealed. I never wanted this to happen to Olive. Poor, poor Olive." Scarlett stood up. "How can I ever atone for my crime? All I ever wanted was to act, to be an artist adored the world over." Her head bowed and her shoulders slumped. "But I am a devil. A murderess." She flung herself to the counter, outstretched arms knocking over a stack of leaflets. Penny watched as they spilled to the floor.

Chase looked up at the heavens. "Forgive me sister, I never meant to hurt you." She staggered across the floor and dropped back into the chair. "Why couldn't we have been friends? And now, we never will be." She wailed.

Penny felt emotionally drained at having witnessed such a dramatic and ostentatious confession. Susie was scribbling away furiously. Gary Tait went to the sobbing Ms Scarlett in a clumsy attempt to comfort the distressed killer. Penny saw the actress sneak a peek from the crook of her arm. As Gary slipped an awkward arm over her shoulder, she cried some more.

"Gary Tait," Cheryl screeched. "You get away from that murderer right now."

Penny saw Cheryl had her phone, and it was already ringing out. It was answered a second later.

"PC Bolton, it's Cheryl Tait at Thatchings. I've found Mrs Sharp's killer. One of our guests here has just confessed it all to me. I suggest you get here right away and arrest her."

Cheryl ended the call then grabbed a decorative poker from the fireplace in the reception area and held it two handed over Chase Scarlett. "Wait outside, Gary, and take Mrs Hughes and Miss Finch with you."

Gary did as his wife told him, and Penny wondered sadly if there had ever been a time when he hadn't. Outside, the day was bright and sunny, with a few fluffy white clouds scudding across a blue sky. Penny could hear the rise and fall of a sustained bout of sobbing coming from inside.

Gary looked at Penny. He was even paler than usual.

"A murderer. I can't believe we've had a murderer staying at Thatchings. What a day."

Penny had never heard a confession like it. The story made sense, but she was far from impressed with the theatrics. Susie was still scribbling and Gary was leaning against the dry stone wall of the property in a daze, so Penny walked Fischer round the garden until she saw PC Bolton pull up and enter the premises. He came out a short while later with Chase Scarlett in handcuffs.

"I take it you want to get to the police station?" Penny said to Susie as they watched PC Bolton's car disappear over the horizon. "I've just got enough time to drop you off in town and get back to Thistle Grange."

"Brilliant. Thanks, Penny. Wow, the *'Coffee Killer Confession.'* That's another scoop for this reporter thanks to you, my brilliant friend."

Leaving an animated Susie at the police station, Penny drove back to her next library stop. She was convinced that even if she and Susie hadn't turned up at Thatchings, Chase Scarlett would probably have confessed to someone else. While the confession had been completely over the top to the point of being almost scripted, there was no doubt the woman was overwhelmed with guilt.

It appeared to be a clear-cut case. An argument between sisters-in-law over a modest family fortune had resulted in an accident and a tragic death. Life in Hampsworthy Downs could now, thankfully, return to normal.

Six

Wednesday afternoon in Thistle Grange and Penny could not get Chase Scarlett's overblown performance out of her mind. She was in danger of drifting off as her customers spoke to her and had to make a concerted effort to concentrate.

As she chatted with library patrons, she heard the clip clop sound of horse hooves approaching the village and a class from the nearby stables rode into view. Young trainee riders mixed in with the more experienced, all heading to the bridal path which eventually gave way to cantering and galloping areas. The sound of them walking along was hypnotic, and Penny felt her eyelids turn heavy.

Fischer became excited and Penny was about to clip on his lead, thinking he wanted to run alongside, then realised he was waiting for his friends.

Mr Sheridan came into view along with Gatsby and Daisy, two fabulous black Labradors who greeted Fischer with joyous barks and play bows, and for a few minutes it was canine chaos as they gamboled, frolicked, and romped. The two dogs were growing fast and already much bigger than Fischer, but he was unperturbed and raced around playing chase, dodging and weaving until all three of them collapsed in a happy heap by the library.

Penny filled a large bowl of water for them. "They're growing so fast, Mr Sheridan," Penny said, scratching the ears of both dogs.

"Full of energy too," he said, looking proudly at his dogs. "They keep me fit and active. Young as well, probably. I don't know what I'd do without them."

Penny kept an eye on the dogs while Mr Sheridan stepped up into the van to look for a book. He glanced at the shelves before turning to Penny.

"I can't quite believe the news from Rowan Downs. It's shocking. Poor Mrs Sharp. I heard Stokes the builder is the prime suspect and has been hauled in for questioning?"

"That's partly correct. I think he's just helping the police get a better picture of what happened that night."

"I heard he stormed the shop when it was full of customers and started shouting about how he was going to kill her before the night was through. That she'd never live to see another day."

Penny rolled her eyes. "It wasn't quite like that. You know what happens in these villages with each new telling of a story, it gets exaggerated and before long it bears absolutely no resemblance to the original. It's Chinese Whispers, Mr

Sheridan. All he wanted was to be paid for some work he'd done for her. But you know what Terry Stokes is like, he's incapable of asking nicely and politely. So yes, he was loud and aggressive but I doubt he threatened to kill her."

"Yes, you're probably right. I take everything I hear with a pinch of salt, anyway. So you don't think Terry is the murderer?"

"No, I don't. But just between us I have just witnessed the most dramatic of confessions from an actress. It won't be a secret for long as it happened at Thatchings and Susie Hughes was with me."

"What actress?"

"Chase Scarlett. She was the star of those coffee adverts years ago, if star is the right word."

"The coffee lady?" Mr Sheridan said. "Gosh, I remember her on the TV. I heard a rumour she was in this neck of the woods, but thought it was highly unlikely and someone had got their wires crossed. And she's now confessed to murder, you say?"

"It turns out she's Mr Sharp's sister. She was called Beryl before she changed her name to seek her fame and fortune. Olive was her sister-in-law, and she's confessed to killing her in an argument about her share of the money from the shop."

"Good grief. Who would have thought Mr Sharp would have had a famous sister? And what would a successful actress want with a chip shop?" Mr Sheridan asked, resuming his perusal of the book shelves.

"She didn't want the shop, just her share of the profits. She was successful once but I haven't seen her in so much as a day time drama since the coffee adverts, and they must have been twenty years ago."

Mr Sheridan nodded. "Fallen on hard times, you think? Yes, that makes sense. So not Terry Stokes then? He is such an uncouth bully I felt sure it was him."

"You and the rest of the villages, probably. He is a bully and appears to be angry all the time but somehow I don't think he's a murderer." Penny said, stroking Gatsby's head as he laid it on her knee.

"Well, all this news has got me in the mood for a good thriller, Penny. Can you suggest one?"

"Top shelf, third from the right," she said immediately. Not wanting to disturb Gatsby. "The latest Kim Stanley Robinson. It has an environmental theme."

Mr Sheridan turned the book over and nodded approvingly. "Thank you. I'll give it a go. The environment is a big topic these days, and rightfully so, but our local environment is just as important. Environmental protection begins at home, you might say. I am not at all happy about this proposed development in Rowan Downs. If anything is going to ruin our local area, it's a huge building site."

Penny shifted Gatsby, who went and flopped down next to his sister and Fischer, and proceeded to check out the book while Mr Sheridan continued. "Only Mrs Sharp was stopping these developers from going ahead. Now the shop will be up for sale and they will swoop in. We really must organise some sort of resident's campaign to stop it. We can't have the area overrun with commuters. If it was for locals, then that would be a different matter, they should be able to find a home here and it would be a much more sympathetic proposal we'd all see to that, but turning the village into a bedroom for city workers is not expanding the community. It will drive prices up beyond the reach of the next generations which will be dreadful news. The heart of the community will be lost forever then."

"My dad is of the same opinion. You should get in touch with him. I'm sure he'd be happy to talk to you about setting up a residents association if you're serious about it?"

"I might just do that. Thanks for the book, Penny. See you next week. Daisy, Gatsby come on." He whistled, and the dogs jumped up to follow. Fischer looked longingly after them.

"Don't look so sad, Fish Face, I'll arrange a proper play date for you soon."

The afternoon clouded over and it looked as though rain was on the horizon, but a strong wind came and blew the clouds away, leaving bright sunshine in its wake. Luckily it was a bit cooler. It had been overly warm recently and the fresher breeze was very welcome.

As Penny packed away the camper van at the end of her busy afternoon, she spotted Terry Stokes parked in his van across the road. He was scrolling through his phone, a pair of half-moon glasses perched on the end of his nose. For such a large man the small spectacles looked incongruous, in fact they were so comical Penny accidentally let out a short laugh. She looked up again just in time to see him snatch the glasses off his nose, eyes fixed firmly on her.

His initial embarrassment quickly turned to anger as he put his glasses away, snapping them in a little case and throwing them aggressively onto the cluttered dashboard, where they disappeared among newspapers, pie wrappers, invoices and assorted paperwork. He glowered at Penny, then pushed open his van door, litter falling to the ground like confetti, and marched across the road toward her.

"Penny Finch, I've got a bone to pick with you," he growled.

Penny stood her ground. She was not afraid of Terry Stokes. He was all bark and no bite and she knew it.

"Terry, don't speak to me like that, please try to keep it civil."

Fischer came to her heel, his front paws digging into the ground, head low and hackles raised, a low snarl starting in his throat.

Stokes gave the little dog a glance, then stopped several feet away. He pointed a fat, grubby finger at her, jabbing each word as he spoke.

"I don't know who you think you are sticking your nose in other people's business, but I'm sick of it. And now you're getting your boyfriend to question people for you, just because you like to spread all the local gossip and fancy yourself as some sort of detective."

"Boyfriend?" Penny said, confused. She was single. Maybe he meant Edward? But they'd ended their relationship a few months ago. "Not that it's any of your business, Terry, but Edward and I have been separated for a while now."

"Edward? That pencil neck?" Stokes scoffed. "Not him, Finch. I'm talking about your police detective boyfriend. John Monroe."

Penny's mouth fell open. What was he talking about? She wasn't in a relationship with DI Monroe. Some people couldn't see that men and women could just be friends. Oh no, there had to be something else going on. Terry Stokes was obviously one of those obtuse people. She didn't find that surprising when she thought about it. For all his bluff and bluster and hard man act he was very immature.

"DI Monroe?" was all she managed to say.

"Yes, him. Having me hauled in for questioning by that ridiculous excuse for a copper, Bolton. Just because I tore a strip of old Sharp for not paying me for that house door I put on for her. The miserly old trout. I'm not surprised she got battered. But it wasn't me and I'll thank you to tell your boyfriend to leave me out of it," he sneered.

He turned on his heel and stormed back to his van.

Penny called out after him when her voice returned.

"You've got it all wrong, Terry."

Stokes shook his head and opened the van door, the wind pulling slips of paper and other assorted detritus out with it. He slammed the door shut and fired the engine, a huge belch of black exhaust smoke exploding into the clean air and drifting away on the breeze as he drove away. He didn't look in his mirrors once before pulling out onto the road.

Penny watched him go, shaking her head in disbelief at the ludicrous assumption. Then realised what Terry had said. "Come on, Fischer, we need to see the back of that shop."

Parked in the small car-park at the back of Chips Ahoy, Penny frowned at the building. There was no new security door fitted either at the front or at the back of the shop. So what work had Terry actually done for Mrs Sharp?

"I think I'll give Mr Kelly a call," Penny told Fischer.

He answered on the third ring.

"Penny, you just caught me."

"Are you going out, Mr Kelly? I won't keep you I just have a quick question."

"Actually, we're going away for a few days. Laura's just loading the car. What can I do for you?"

"Did Mrs Sharp live above the shop, do you know? Only Terry said he fitted a security door and I assumed it was here. But there's no sign of one front or back."

"Is there not? I took it for granted it was at the shop too. But, no she doesn't live there the flat above is used for storage, I believe. The Sharps bought a house from old Mr Pike when they first moved to Rowan Downs."

"Pike as in Pikes Farm?"

"That's right. It actually was part of the farm at one point I think but was sold off."

"So, it's near the farm?"

"Yes, along the same road on the left, just after the turning to Thornehurst Grange. It's the only house along there. Quite isolated as it's surrounded by fields but the garden is lovely. You can't miss it."

Penny heard a car horn toot in the background.

"I'll let you go, Mr Kelly. Have a lovely break with your family."

"I will, Penny, I'm sure. And do let me know what you find out, even though you're not actually investigating."

Penny laughed and hung up the phone, restarting the engine. She knew exactly where the house was now. She and Mr Kelly had visited Major Colton at Thornehurst Grange over Christmas when they were investigating the death of a local woman.

Driving to Pikes Cross she turned left and not long after passing the turn off to Major Colton's she spied a single house on the left-hand side of the road. With no other building in sight and the road culminating in a dead end at Pikes Farm, she knew this must be the Sharp's home.

The front of the house had an established garden, with the building set back from the road in the middle of the plot. There was a gate, but nowhere for Penny to park. She slowly drove along the privet hedge which fronted the property and found a small side road. She turned in and parked the van. With Fischer on his lead, they walked up the slight hill of the track and found another to the rear running parallel with the house and the main road, which brought them to the back gate. Again, the gardens were quite large and well established. She opened the wooden gate and walked the length of the path to the back door. A brand new security door stared out at her.

"So he fitted it here," Penny mused. "I wonder why she felt she needed it?" Fischer sat at her heel, gazing up at her as though he understood every word. "I mean, granted the place is isolated, but she's lived here for years. Why the sudden need for a door like this?"

She sauntered up the path, deep in thought, and turned to look back at the house. The place looked deserted now, with all the curtains drawn. Fischer gave a little whine, eager to explore.

"I think it's safe to let you off here, Fish Face."

She unclipped his lead and the little dog went tearing around the lawns and under bushes seeking out new smells while Penny broached the ground-floor window. Cupping hands over her eyes, she tried to look inside, but there wasn't even one small chink in the curtain giving a view of the interior. She moved to the next window, but it was the same story. She'd learn nothing this way.

Deciding to double check the front door, she found the path culminated in a solid stone built porch with a sturdy front door. The small glass panel at the top showed another door, again strong and solid, which would lead into the house. No chance of getting through those two, Penny thought.

She reversed her route and found Fischer digging under a bush halfway up the path.

"Fischer, no don't dig." She ran over and quickly clipped on his lead. "Come on, little man, time to go home. There's nothing here for us."

Later that evening Fischer was out in Penny's cottage garden waiting, although this time she knew what he was waiting for. The little dog was obviously craving Mrs Sharp's unique batter.

"You need to forget all about it, Fish Face," Penny said as she accompanied him on his patrol around the garden. "Susie won't be giving you anymore scraps. The chip shop is closed and I don't know if it will ever open again. And even if it does, I doubt the chips or the batter will be the same. That family recipe has gone with her I'm afraid. I'm sorry, Little man, but you are going to have to go cold turkey on this batter addiction you have."

Penny wondered what had been so special about the Chips Ahoy batter that had people so hooked on it. She'd never tried it. Being a vegetarian she didn't eat bought fish and chips. She made her own batter for courgette rings or mushrooms and added salt and pepper, but that was a standard recipe. A beer batter was also popular, in fact The Pig and Whistle pub served beer batter cod, huge pieces of fish that hung over the side of the plate. But there was nothing unique about it. It had to be something else. Unfortunately, it was unlikely she'd ever know what it was now. Irritating as it was, it would have to be one mystery she'd never solve.

She yawned as she got ready for bed. It had been a long and event filled day. Tomorrow was the last day of her week, a library stop in her own village, Cherrytree Downs, in the morning and then over to the main library at Winstoke to restock.

"We must remember to take Edward his book," Penny said to Fischer. He let out a little whine in response. "Don't worry, we won't stay long. I'll drop it off then we'll leave." She swore the little dog smiled at her.

She walked through to the kitchen and put the kettle on. She'd take a cup of tea to bed and curl up with a book, although it was likely her eyes would close before she even got through the first pages. She was exhausted.

She dug in the cupboard for the new box of fennel tea. It was not a tea she had tried before, the one she'd made by mistake this morning she hadn't drunk, but it apparently settled the stomach and calmed the body. It tasted a little like licorice according to the box, with a relaxing scent and had a slightly bitter after taste if brewed too long. But Penny would only make a weak one. As she pulled the box from the cupboard and opened it, Fischer spun round a couple of times and hopped on his back legs pawing at her knee. Tail wagging in a blur.

"Since when did you like tea, Fischer?" Penny laughed. "Oh, I see, your treats are in the same cupboard, aren't they?" She gave the little dog a bone shaped chew, but he dropped it to the floor without eating it, his concentration wholly on the tea.

"Wait a minute. You wanted this tea this morning, didn't you? So that's what this is all about, is it? You've got a taste for Fennel," Penny said to the little dog. "Well, you can't have anymore in tea, but I'm sure I can find you a proper dog treat which has it. This must have been part of Mrs Sharp's secret batter recipe. Well done, Fischer, another mystery solved."

With the tea made, she climbed the stairs with Fischer hot on her heels and got into bed with a relieved sigh. Fischer jumped up beside her and curled up, head on her shoulder and tail thumping on the duvet.

"Just one chapter," she said with a huge yawn as she opened the book. But she didn't make it further than page three before her eyes closed, and tea forgotten, she drifted into a dreamless sleep.

Seven

On Thursday morning Penny was woken up by a loud thump as the book she'd been reading the night before fell to the floor. She must have fallen asleep mid chapter. It was a sound that greeted her quite often. She leaned over the side of her bed, a sliver of sun streaming in over the bedroom floor from a crack in the curtains, and scooped up her fallen book, giving a sleepy Fischer a kiss on his nose before retreating back under the duvet to find her place. She read a few pages before it was finally time to get up.

Thursday was always a good day, as the library didn't have to go far. It meant she could grab a few more minutes in bed. It was the last day of the working week and she always felt a little lighter, more relaxed. She looked forward to catching up and sharing news with her colleagues at the main library in town and seeing what new books had come in that she could recommend to her customers.

In many ways it was the hardest day of the week, but every day had its own challenges and rewards. Thursday however was special, even Fischer was more enthusiastic on a Thursday. Although that was probably due to the treats he knew her colleagues would have waiting for him. Everybody loved Fischer.

"Come on, Fish Face, that's enough slouching around we need to get a move on."

It was only a short drive from her front door to her library pitch on the village green. It was another beautiful blue sky day with the odd cloud floating lazily over the sun. Penny set up her table and chair, part of a camping set she'd owned for years, and made a cup of tea for herself and poured a bowl of water for Fischer, giving him his morning treat while she waited for her first patrons. No doubt he'd get several more as the day wore on.

She was right. Before long a familiar customer arrived to return her book and select a new one, hand reaching into her cardigan pocket for a dog biscuit. Fischer sat and gave his paw to shake, then barked a thank you after he'd finished it.

It seemed every customer who came by had a treat for the little dog. He was a source of entertainment and happiness for many of the elderly who came to library. Few of the older generation travelled far now and visiting the library was a big social event for them. Penny was happy to be of service.

Just as she checked out a stack of books for one of her regulars, her mobile rang. Before she even glanced at the screen, some sixth sense told her it would be Susie.

"Hi, Susie. If it's another lift you need, you'll have to hang on for a little while. I haven't had all my regulars turn up yet and can't leave until I've seen them. Can you wait? I'm nearly finished." Penny said.

"No, I don't need a lift today," Susie said excitedly. "I'm at the garage, just waiting for my car now. Another few minutes and I will be mobile again and then I can offer you a lift. If you trust my driving that is."

Penny smiled. "There's nothing wrong with your driving," she fibbed smoothly. She really didn't want to be a passenger while Susie was behind the wheel, unless it was a life or death situation. It wasn't that she was a bad driver, she was just fast. Not actually speeding or breaking the rules, just hectic. Always dashing here and there, or worse in town, where she'd suddenly dive down a side street or take a narrow back alley. Susie always sat forward in her seat, eyes darting this way and that, looking for a chance to beat the traffic. She would have made an excellent rally driver. "So, what can I do for you?"

"Just calling for a chat, really." Susie said.

Penny recognised that tone, her friend had something interesting to tell her but was delaying. Penny played along.

"I've got time for a casual chat."

"Hang on, the mechanic wants me."

Penny could hear a murmured conversation in the background, then Susie came back on the line.

"They said the car was ready, so I dashed over to pick it up and now they're telling me there's a filter needs changing or something. I've told my boss I'll be an hour late, and it's almost an hour now. I'll get sacked if I don't come up with a great story for the weekend edition."

"No you won't, Susie. Your boss thinks too much of you for that."

"Yeah, maybe. So, how's your morning going?"

Penny sipped her tea. She looked across the village green toward the duck pond, the sun shimmering on the water. A customer was comparing two books, one in each hand, almost weighing them up for size. To be honest, Penny's morning was absolutely ideal. She couldn't wish for anything more or better. Susie had a job, which by comparison was far more glamorous, not Hollywood reporter glamorous, but she was always out and about gathering information and interviewing people for a worthwhile story that would have the locals talking. But for all the excitement of Susie's job, Penny wouldn't swap hers for anything.

"Oh, my morning is going fine. Books in, books out. You know how it is." She took another sip of tea, patiently waiting for Susie to tell her what was going on. There was a silence at the other end of the phone. "All right enough prevaricating, Hughes. I know you've got news, spill the beans."

Susie laughed. "Gotcha! Well, I've been doing a bit of digging."

"Go on, Sherlock, what have found out?"

"The land Eddie Tompkins' caravan is sitting on is in his name. He owns it, Penny. He bought it in the early 90s, before he even moved to the area. Then, years later there was a planning application made and granted for a housing development. Permission has been in place for almost three years but it will elapse if not used within that time frame."

Penny was astounded. She never for one minute thought Eddie Tompkins owned the land he was living on, she thought he had either squatter's rights or permission from the real owner.

"And," Susie went on. "There is one other name on the planning application. A local. I bet you can't guess who it is?"

Penny put her cup down and sat upright. A mystery. Who? She wracked her brains. Who could possibly have gone into partnership with Eddie Tompkins? She knew she only had seconds before Susie blurted out the name. She felt the time ticking down and the dramatic music rising like the clock from the quiz show Countdown.

"Terry Stokes," Susie said triumphantly. "Stokes and Tompkins agreed a business deal but for some reason the work never started. One of them is obviously blocking the development from going ahead. The planning permission will expire soon and if the work hasn't started by then it will be void and a fresh application will have to be made. Who knows whether it will be granted a second time? And, as we both know, the field runs adjacent to the Chips Ahoy building, it would be easy enough to expand the application to include that."

"So that's why the two of them don't get on, a business deal gone sour." Penny said.

"Maybe Eddie wants to protect his field? Keep it as it is and maintain the natural beauty of the area?"

Penny didn't need to think that suggestion over. "Then why would he go into the deal in the first place? I doubt he wants to look after the field and the wildlife, Susie, if the amount of poor rabbits hanging on his line is anything to go by. I doubt Eddie would pass up the opportunity to make some money. If he's prepared to eat left over chip shop scraps and murder the wildlife, then I think he'd be equally prepared to ruin our environment for a hefty payout."

"I'm not so sure about that, actually. Oh, I've got to run, Penny, my car is ready."

"Okay. Drive safe, Susie, and well done on the investigation."

"Thanks. What are you doing later, by the way? It's pub quiz night and we've come so close to beating Universally Challenged and Artificial Intelligence in the last competitions. Only five points in it last time. What do you say?"

"I say we need a much better quiz team name. Penny and Susie isn't very imaginative coming from a writer and a librarian."

"I'll come up with a name and you can get the first round in. Right, I really have got to go. See you later."

Penny ended the call and tapped her phone on her chin, deep in thought.

"Stokes and Tompkins. Who would have thought?" she muttered quietly before slipping her phone away and greeting her latest customer.

Penny enjoyed a steady morning with interesting people and even more interesting book choices. It was almost a pity that after a great morning she had to pack up. This was the last session of the week and it ended with the usual sense of a job well done and a slight regret it was all over. All she had to do now was to spend the afternoon in the Winstoke library building, restocking the camper van for the following week, depositing fines and catching up with Emma and Sam.

She closed the side doors and got behind the wheel. "What have I forgotten, Fischer?" she said, looking down at her bright eyed companion. She was sure there was something she needed to do. Fischer let out a little yap, the one he used when he needed to go out.

"Do you need to go out for a minute?"

Fischer lay down on the seat and put his paw over his nose. It was the position he had used regularly when Edward visited.

"Fischer, you are the cleverest little dog I have ever known. Good boy!"

She gave him a kiss on the head and a treat from his stash in the glove compartment.

"Of course, Edward's book. I've left it on the hall table at home. Come on, it will be quicker to walk."

They jumped out of the van and walked through the village to her cottage. The Art of War had been sitting in the hall all week waiting for her to pick it up. But it had blended into the background. Much like her relationship with its owner.

Maybe subconsciously she hadn't forgotten to pick it up. Perhaps she'd tried to ignore it because there was a large part of her who didn't want to see Edward. To see him would be to remember their time together and how it had ended. She'd not been upset when they'd gone their separate ways. The relationship had stalled a long time ago and had been going nowhere, with neither of them happy. It was more the fact he'd cheated on her. It was the deceit and the betrayal that had hurt the most.

Penny stood in the hallway staring at the book, then realised she was wasting time. She snatched it up. At the garden gate she hesitated by the bin, which was partially hidden by a wicker screen and an overgrown honeysuckle. No, she couldn't throw a book away. It was sacrilege. What sort of librarian would that make her? She'd just have to bite the bullet and get on with it.

"Come on, Fischer, the quicker we get there the quicker we can leave."

Fischer barked in agreement.

Penny took the only exit from the village and drove along the road, skirting the bottom of Sugar Hill. As she reached the entrance to Rowan Downs, she saw the closed up Chips Ahoy. A few days ago it would have been a hive of activity during lunch, with a queue of eager customers waiting to be served and the outdoor seating area packed with people. Now it stood quiet and forlorn. She turned left onto the main Winstoke road, shaking her head in sadness.

As she travelled, she glanced out of the window at Tompkins' field and spied Terry Stokes' van. It was parked in a small lay-by next to the gate she and Susie had climbed over two days ago. On impulse she slowed down, indicating, then pulled over to the right side of the road, next to the hedge that separated the field from the main road. Clipping on Fischer's lead, she jumped out and walked along the hedge, stepping over the grass verge until she reached the corner where she knew Eddie's caravan was sitting. She pressed a finger to her lips, telling Fischer not to make a sound. She could hear raised voices from the other side.

"I won't tell you again, Terry, get off my land. You are not digging it up and that's the end of it."

"We had a deal, you scruffy good-for-nothing hippie."

"I changed my mind a long time ago. You can't cover it with concrete without my agreement and I won't give it. This field is too beautiful to die, it must be protected."

"You couldn't give a tinker's cuss about this field, Ed, and we both know it," Terry growled. "I'll have this field off you one day, you mark my words."

"Over my dead body," Tompkins said.

Then Penny heard a sound that sent a confused shiver down her spine. Terry Stokes and Eddie Tompkins were chuckling together.

"Just forget it, Terry. I made trouble for you before, I can do it again."

"It was you?" Stokes said in surprise. "I thought it was that snooping little librarian who'd been talking to the police. There'll be another murder round here if you try something like that again, you old tramp."

"I didn't tell them I saw you," Eddie replied casually. "I said I saw someone. It's not my fault you look like a thug."

Penny heard a heavy thud, and Eddie let out a yelp.

"Get off my land, Stokes, or else."

"Or else what?"

Penny listened, straining to hear, but there was nothing but silence. Then Terry spoke.

"I'm digging up this field, Eddie. You'll have to do much better than trying to get me locked up. I won't change my mind; it's just a matter of time. So sort out your grubby little caravan, clear up your business and clear off, or I'll be the one talking to the police."

"We both know you won't do that, Terry."

Penny peered through the thick hedgerow. She could just make out the corner of the caravan and then she saw movement as Terry Stokes trudged off along the field trail, while Eddie moved back to his abode, nursing a split lip.

Penny straightened up, and she and Fischer ran back to the van. They jumped in, and she quickly turned the key. The motor whirred, but the engine failed to burst into life.

"Oh no, don't die on me now."

She glanced nervously in the rear-view mirror. It would only take Terry a few minutes to get to the gate and see her. She took a deep breath and turned the ignition key again.

The engine roared into life. "Oh, thank goodness." She glanced in the side mirror, indicating but there was a car coming. She was desperate to put her foot down and pull out in front of it so Terry didn't see her, but it was too near and travelling too fast. She let the other vehicle go first, then pulled out after it. Checking her rear-view mirror, she saw Terry Stokes, hands on hips and a mean scowl on his face as he watched her drive away.

Penny concentrated on the road. Fischer was standing, paws on the dashboard. No matter how well trained he was she didn't think he'd take to wearing a seat belt. She told him to sit on his seat, which he did. At least that was safer for him.

She couldn't shake the image of Stokes staring after her van. Was he aware she'd been eavesdropping on his conversation with Eddie? Probably. She concentrated on the road and tried to put it out of her mind.

Fischer panted and woofed happily all the way to town. His good mood infected Penny so that by the time they arrived at the library, they both had a spring in their step.

The library was one of the best environments Penny could imagine. She'd come here often as a young girl, always pestering her parents to bring her at every opportunity. Immediately as she walked in, she felt as though she'd come home.

She'd loved the library at university, the dark tall wooden shelves making quirky corners, hidden alcoves and secret nooks to lose yourself in when studying, all the while surrounded by old books. Most of her studies could have been done in the brightly lit computer rooms, but she always preferred the old stacks.

Winstoke library was slightly more modern than her old uni library. Although there was a hushed and respectful atmosphere for those reading, it was not deathly quiet. There was life here. The colonel was sitting in the study area poring over a large reference book of naval ships. At the opposite end of the table, a pair of local boys were studying for a school assignment. The ladies of the knitting circle were chatting in hushed tones, their occasional giggles rising above the peace. The children's book club was in a small activity room acting out a scene from a book being read to them by a visiting story teller.

Emma and Sam were chatting animatedly at the main desk. Emma saw Penny first and beamed.

"Penny, we've been reading this new mystery. We've kept a copy back for you, it's right up your street I'd say." Emma crouched down and gave Fischer a hug and a huge fuss as he walked behind the counter.

"Oh, that looks great." Penny said as she took the proffered book from Emma. "Thanks, you two."

"You'll have to read fast, even by your standards, to catch up with Emma on this one," Sam said. He also stooped to say hello to the little dog and produced a treat from his pocket. Fischer shook paws in thanks.

Emma laughed. "We've been matching each other page for page but Sam didn't read last night..."

"I had to fix a leaking shower head at home. It's been driving me up the wall. Drip, drip, drip all night long. I've been putting it off for weeks thinking I'd mess it up and have a flood on my hands. But it only took half an hour and was easy." He turned to Penny, jabbing a thumb in Emma's direction. "And now Miss Competitive here, she's a few pages ahead and taunting me. She's been threatening me with spoilers all morning."

"She'd never do it, Sam. It's one of the unwritten rules of the library." Penny said.

Penny sorted through the library van returns with Emma and Sam, enjoying their enthusiasm for the new book. They were very careful not to give away any details, but from what they did say it sounded like a perfect book for her to lose herself in for a few nights.

With the returns completed and the library restocked for the following week, and Mr Gregory's fine deposited in the till, Penny's week was done. Tomorrow she and Fischer would have a day to themselves.

"Tea, anyone?" Penny said.

Fischer went and curled up in his library bed, tucked on the bottom shelf behind the counter. At the sound of the word 'tea' he knew he had the chance to grab forty winks.

Emma and Sam both nodded as they checked out books for the children's club. The knitting group was ready to leave too and would be coming up any minute to check out their choices.

Penny moved to the library kitchen, where she washed up a few bits and bobs and left them to dry on the draining board while the kettle boiled. The cupboard above the microwave housed the teapot Penny had brought in for the library staff's use, a large cream one with a multicoloured cupcake design. She warmed it up then threw in some English breakfast tea bags. Not her first choice but they did make a good cup of tea.

She carried the loaded tray back to the counter, where Sam was just seeing off the last of the knitting group. The library was quiet now, apart from the gentle rustle of pages as the colonel leafed through the naval encyclopedia.

"We heard about Mrs Stokes, Penny," Sam said. "I can't believe it. Who'd want to harm an old lady like that?"

Penny shook her head and took a sip of tea. "I don't know, Sam. The police are obviously looking into it."

"Are you?" Emma asked her.

"Well, there are a couple of things that don't make sense to me."

"If anyone can sort it out, you can, Penny," Emma said with conviction. "You've done it before."

Sam nodded in agreement. "And you've got Fischer here. With a nose like his, he'll sniff out the clues you need. You'll both work it out in no time."

Penny wasn't convinced, but smiled anyway. Then talk turned back to the current read.

It was a lovely way to end the week and after a final mouthful of tea, Penny left Sam and Emma to battle over the last biscuit. She picked up the book Emma had already checked out for her and promised to have it finished by the following week so they could all talk about 'whodunit.'

Outside, she turned to Fischer. "Just one more thing to do before we can go home. Let's take Edward his book back."

Fischer shook his body from the tip of his nose all the way down to the end of his tail, then looked up at Penny as if to say, 'I'm ready, let's get it over with.'

"My sentiments exactly, Fish Face."

Penny drove into the private car park and halted next to a large black four wheel drive with silver flames decorating the rear wheel arches. It takes all sorts, she supposed as she eyed the vehicle with amusement. No doubt it belonged to a flash accountant with more money from overbilling his clients than sense.

The offices of Edward's accountancy firm were dull and hushed. Grey carpets and grey walls. Hardly any colour anywhere. Phones were ringing behind grey doors and people beyond were talking in low muted tones. They sounded like automatons, Penny thought with a shudder. She stepped up to the reception desk, but there was no one there. Probably just been called away for a moment, Penny presumed. A phone was ringing on the desk, so she expected they would return any second. However, the seconds turned into minutes and still no one came. She waited, book in hand, Fischer sitting at her side.

She had no need to actually see Edward. She could just leave the book at reception with a brief note. It might get delayed in the internal mail system for a while, but he'd waited this long so he obviously wasn't missing it. And if she was being completely honest with herself, she didn't want to bump into the woman Edward had left her for.

The phone behind the reception stopped ringing and there was still no receptionist.

"This isn't a very good way to run a business, is it, Fischer?"

She looked around for someone she could hand the book to, peeking along the grey corridor that ran from reception to the offices, but apart from some insipid watercolour style prints in chrome frames, the corridor held no life at all.

Penny slapped the Art of War on the counter.

"What would Sun Tzu say?" Penny asked her little dog. She opened the book at random.

'Water has no constant shape, nor does battle. Be swift like the wind.' She read aloud. "No help there, and I can't really see how that's supposed to inspire an accountant."

Penny decided to move swiftly like the wind down the corridor, and make her way towards Edward's office.

A half glass wall on one side showed her an office pool where half a dozen bored accountants and support staff were at work. Plastic pot plants and grey partition walls sat at the end of desks. It was busy, she'd expected everyone to be winding down for the end of the day but all the people she saw through the glazed wall were busy tapping on keyboards or speaking on the phone. Maybe they were all trying to look busy while counting down the minutes? Penny suppressed another shudder. It was her idea of hell, no creativity, no colour or warmth. No one was smiling, no office jokes or camaraderie. It felt completely soulless.

Suddenly the receptionist came out of a side door, a stack of papers in her arms. She was impeccably dressed. Tight white blouse, tight grey skirt, her blond hair in a tidy chignon and balancing on a pair of black patent leather shoes with six-inch heels. Designer glasses framed green eyes and arched eyebrows and sat above a petite nose and red lips.

Penny was suddenly acutely aware of her own work attire. A loose patterned blouse, white with pink rosebuds, a pink cardigan and cropped jeans with sandals. She suddenly felt very under-dressed.

The office woman looked Penny up and down. A slight arch of a well plucked eyebrow suggested she didn't approve of her attire, but worse there was a hint of amusement tinged with pity. She glanced at Fischer, who was being on his best behaviour and looking very cute, and pulled a face.

"Can I help you?" She paused, "Madam?"

Madam? Penny heard the word like an insult. The young office girl might as well have called her an old maid.

Penny straightened her shoulders and took a deep breath, mustering all her confidence, determined not to feel inferior. "I'm here to see Edward Marshall."

The woman nodded and pointed a scarlet fingernail along the corridor to an office door at the far end which looked exactly like all the others.

"He's with a client at the moment. Just take a seat round the corner." She gave Penny a final measured look, then tottered back toward reception.

Penny couldn't help but admire Edward. He'd wanted promotion more than anything, including a relationship with her. Now he had his wish. Not only did he have an office of his own, but a plush seating area for his important clients.

A low black faux leather sofa was partially obscured by a towering plastic tree with waxy looking green leaves and a brown furry trunk. Possibly modelled after an existing plant, but more likely a contrivance because Penny had never seen anything remotely similar in the real world. There was a glass topped coffee table with chrome legs strewn with copies of Accountancy Quarterly, the subtitle, 'It all adds up.'

She went to the sofa but then was struck by a wave of defiance. She wasn't going to wait any longer, she had things to do. She strode to the office door and knocked.

"One moment," Edward's voice said from inside.

Penny overheard him talking to someone.

"You are heavily invested, Mr Snipe. If the development can go ahead imminently, then you will make it through without any worries of insolvency. However, if the work is stalled for any reason, then the contractor's agreement means they will be owed a portion of the fee and unfortunately that will take Snipe Developments into the red."

Penny noticed Fischer standing next to a coat stand, licking the cuffs of a jacket hanging off the lowest peg.

"What are you doing, Fischer?" Penny whispered. She guided the little dog away and made him sit next to her.

"How deep in the red will I be, Edward?" The client's voice said, rasping and reedy, but just loud enough to be heard by Penny on the other side of the door.

"I'll be honest with you, Mr Snipe. Very deep, I'm afraid. I can't see any way for the company to survive another failed development."

"I have a feeling things will start to move ahead quite quickly now. Keep juggling until then, Edward, would you?"

Fischer had once again stood up and was straining at the lead, trying to get back the jacket. Penny was about to knock again, then thought better of it. She'd waited long enough. She pushed open the door.

"Edward," she said, mustering a cheery voice and a bright smile. "Only me. I won't keep you, I can see you're busy."

Edward looked at Penny in shock. Opening and closing his mouth a few times before he found his voice.

"Penny?"

She stepped in, bringing Fischer with her. Edward's client, Snipe, was pacing back and forth in front of the window, wearing a blue crumpled suit and a frown above a messy ginger moustache. He looked somewhat familiar, but she didn't have time to work out where she'd seen him before because Fischer dashed into the office so fast the lead slipped out of Penny's hand. She had never seen her little dog so elated at meeting a stranger. He jumped up, dancing on his back legs, tail wagging furiously. The client recoiled.

"What the heck is this, Edward?" Snipe said, backing away from Fischer with his hands in the air.

"I'm so sorry, Mr Snipe. Penny, can't you control that animal for once?" he snapped.

These were the first words Edward had spoken to her in weeks, and it was to berate her. She refused to pass the scolding onto her little dog. She looked at Mr Snipe, who was staring in horrified fascination at Fischer, who was leaping about, tongue lolling as he huffed in excitement.

"I think he likes you," Penny said, amused.

"I don't like dogs."

"Penny, wait outside, please." Edward said with barely controlled fury. "I'm in a very important meeting with Mr Snipe."

Penny took hold of Fischer's lead and gently but firmly pulled him away from Mr Snipe.

"I apologise, Mr Snipe. He usually waits to be introduced before making a fuss of someone like that."

Penny looked at Fischer, still pulling like crazy to get back to Snipe. She couldn't understand what had got into him.

"We are all done here, Edward," Snipe said. "I'll see myself out."

He swept past Penny, avoiding Fischer's lunge for his leg, exited the office and grabbing the jacket on the stand outside, marched away.

Edward moved behind his office desk, hand on his hips and a look of anger on his face.

"What the heck was that all about, Penny? Don't you know how important that client is? What are you doing here?"

"I just wanted to return your book. The Art of War." She held the copy up and Edward's face changed completely. A bright smile replacing the pinched lips.

"There it is. I wondered where it had got to. I've been looking for it for weeks. I didn't think I'd left it at your place. It's a good job I didn't borrow it from the library or I'd be stung with a hefty one pound fine for a late return." He laughed loudly. "I'm not sure I could remain solvent if I had to do that. But at least the local economy would be back in the black." He chuckled again, not caring, or probably not noticing, that Penny didn't find him funny.

"I can't believe after months of not seeing each other you're still making these same lame jokes, Edward. Regardless of what you think, and believe me your opinion matters not, the library is a vital service for the villages. You know very well the fines are more symbolic than for any financial consideration. But they do help to keep us going."

Edward became cross and sullen. He wasn't used to Penny answering back, nor being told his opinion was worthless.

"You may as well just give books away. What a waste of time and money. If it wasn't for the likes of my client Simon Snipe, the local economy would be in ruin."

"It sounded like he was going bust from where I was standing," Penny retorted.

"Were you eavesdropping on confidential conversations, Penny?" Edward shook his head. "Still snooping at every opportunity I see. But for your information he has put everything on the line to try to improve things around here and when he completes the commuter village, money will flood into Hampsworthy Downs. Enough to buy your ridiculous old mobile library hundreds of times over."

"He's the man behind Snipe Developments? I expected someone bigger and more rugged for a builder." Penny said. She'd seen the odd advertising hoarding around the town.

"Don't be so obtuse. He doesn't carry bricks up and down the ladder himself, he has employees for that. He's the boss. The brains." Edward said, tapping his temple. "If it wasn't for men like him, there would be no buildings at all."

"Well, I for one hope it fails. The last thing Rowan Downs needs, or any of the villages in the area for that matter, is a load of commuters clogging up the roads with their big cars and putting pressure on the infrastructure."

Edward tutted loudly and shook his head slowly. "Snipe can help the area build and grow. And now the chip shop has closed, he might be able to buy that old building, too. The area needs more modern housing for professionals not an old fish and chip shop that's seen better days."

Penny dropped the Art of War on his desk and walked away. She was at a loss as to what she had ever seen in Edward Marshall.

"Sadly, I can't say it's been a pleasure, Edward."

"Shut the door on your way out, Pen."

Penny gritted her teeth. She hated being called Pen, and he knew it. He was obviously doing it to annoy her. It was petty. Well, two could play at that game. She deliberately left the door open.

On the way out, she saw Simon Snipe leaning on the reception desk ogling the receptionist. He looked up and jumped aside as Fischer darted toward him.

"Sorry. I don't know what's got into him today. You seem to have made an impression." Penny said, pulling Fischer out into the street, much to the little dog's dismay.

Across the car park, Penny could see someone looking through the library van windows. It was not one of her customers, not here in town, and she didn't like their audacity. Spending even a short time with Edward had put Penny in a bad mood. She marched over, determined to give whoever it was a piece of her mind.

Eight

"Just what do you think you're doing?" Penny said icily, marching up behind the man. He practically jumped out of his skin and spun round. It was John Monroe. Penny nearly stumbled.

"Oh, John. I'm sorry I didn't realise it was you. Can I help?"

Monroe smiled. "I saw the library as I drove past."

"Do you want a book?"

"No, I was hoping to have a word if I could?" he bent down and tickled Fischer under the chin as the little dog leaned against his leg.

"Um, yes, of course. What about?"

"I was thinking perhaps you'd like to join me for an early dinner, seeing as you are in town and it's the end of the day. Unless you need to be somewhere else? I know a nice place not far from here if you're interested?"

"No." Penny said firmly.

Monroe twitched. "Oh, right. Okay."

"Sorry. I mean, no, I don't have anywhere to be. That sounds lovely. Do they allow dogs?"

"I'm sure they do," he replied with a grin. "But if not we'll find somewhere that does."

The Red Lion pub in the centre of town had a lovely beer garden at the back and were more than happy to allow Fischer to join them. The waitress even provided a bowl of water for him. They chose a table on the lawn under a tree and Penny ordered a vegetarian pasta dish with a tall glass of lime and lemonade. Monroe said he'd have the same.

"You know you can have a meat dish if you want. I'm not the sort to push my vegetarianism on other people." Penny said.

"I know that, but I'm not the sort to eat meat in front of a vegetarian. Besides, I liked the sound of what you ordered. So, how are you, Penny? You looked a bit cross when you found me at your van."

"Sorry, I'd just been to see Edward."

"Ah, and how is Mr Marshall?"

Penny shrugged, "His usual bombastic self."

Monroe smiled knowingly and nodded. He knew Edward of old as they'd attended Manchester University at the same time, although they'd never been friends. In fact, Edward had been downright rude one evening when John had turned up to check she was all right after receiving a particularly threatening note. Edward had acted like a petulant schoolboy when he'd barged past John on the doorstep without a word, throwing him a nasty glance. Penny still cringed when she thought about it.

"Penny for them," John said, then laughed and shook his head ruefully. "I'm so sorry, that was not meant as a joke."

"I don't think I ever apologised for Edward's rudeness to you that night when you came to check on me."

"Edward is a grown man, Penny. Why do you feel the need to apologise for him?"

She twirled the pasta around her fork, wondering the same thing. "I don't know. I got used to it, I suppose. But this is the last time. I gave him short shrift earlier so I think the rose-tinted glasses have well and truly come off. Fallen to the ground and smashed to pieces too, actually."

"Glad to hear it. You deserve much better."

Penny swallowed and cleared her throat. "Any developments with the case?"

Monroe was about to speak when a couple walked passed their table, bending down to make a fuss of Fischer, who was looking extra adorable in an attempt to get a morsel of their dinner. As soon as they were out of earshot, he leaned towards her.

"I can't have anyone overhearing," he said. "Chase Scarlett didn't do it. We released her earlier today."

"But she confessed. Admittedly it was totally over the top, but I really thought she'd done it? Why on earth would she confess if she was innocent?"

Monroe shook his head. "She definitely had an argument with Mrs Sharp, which included a physical altercation. But we've had the pathology report back. Mrs Sharp had a nasty bang to the head which corresponds with Ms Scarlett's confession, but that wasn't what killed her."

"So, Chase just thought she was responsible?"

"That's right. She must have knocked her out for a moment and ran away in a panic. When she heard Olive was dead, she naturally assumed it was her fault."

"Well, if it wasn't Chase, then who was it?"

John shook his head, taking the last mouthful of his food, and wiped his mouth with a serviette. He leaned back, glass in hand.

"We spoke to Terry Stokes again, but he has an alibi of sorts. He was at home playing on-line poker from 9pm to 2am. His bank details and IP address confirm it. He's guilty of wasting money, but that's not a crime. However, there's a possibility it could be someone he lives with who was using the gambling site. His bank card is attached to the account so it would automatically debit his funds no matter who was playing. There's no way of proving it was Terry physically on-line, even though he says it was. We're keeping an eye on him though."

"What about Eddie Tompkins? Don't you think it was a little strange he was there?"

Monroe suddenly burst out laughing, which took Penny by surprise. She'd never seen him like this before.

"Yes, it could be he was trying to shift the blame onto someone else to cover his own guilt, or to throw us off the scent. Sometimes killers do come forward with information because they can't resist the lure of wanting to be involved. We pay particularly close attention to such people."

Penny nodded. She'd read that more than once in the mystery and thriller novels she was partial to. But that didn't explain the hilarity.

"So, what was so funny?"

"Eddie Tompkins has a solid alibi, including a police report that put him on the road just outside Rowan Downs for much of Sunday night. After he'd picked up his free chips from the shop and before Olive Sharp's time of death, which the pathologist has confirmed."

"What was he doing?"

"Kung Fu yoga in nothing but his underpants." Monroe said, starting to laugh again.

Penny giggled with him. "What?"

"Several reports came in of a half naked man standing at the side of the road doing some kind of weird dance. We dispatched an officer from Winstoke and apparently it's a form of Tai chi meant to be performed under a moonlit sky. In case you aren't aware, it's also known as shadow boxing, an internal Chinese martial art practised for defense training, health benefits and meditation. As far as alibis are concerned it's the most off the wall one I've had yet, but there's no doubt it was Eddie. Takes all sorts I suppose."

Penny found it amusing, bizarre, and more than a little interesting. Eddie Tompkins was an odd duck, that was for sure.

"So, we have a police officer who spoke to Tompkins at the time of Olive Sharp's death, and several witness reports stating he'd been there a while. His clothes were in a heap at the side of the road and were checked thoroughly. We're convinced it was not him." John said.

"You checked his clothes? What for, a murder weapon?"

Penny swirled the last of her tagliatelle through the cream sauce and swallowed it. Pushing her empty dish aside, she picked up her drink and waited for John to answer.

"Mrs Sharp drowned." He said.

"Drowned?" Penny asked, in confusion. "But how?"

"She was held down in a vat of batter," Monroe answered, all signs of humour gone. "The pathologist found batter in her airways meaning she was still alive when held down. And she put up a fight. For an old woman she was stronger than she looked, but I suppose we all would be when fighting for our life. But whoever did it was very determined to see her off and they would have been covered in batter mixture. That vat held a gallon and judging by the residue left, it was full when Mrs Sharp was pushed into it. It went everywhere."

"How awful. Poor Mrs Sharp. I think you're right though, Eddie Tompkins was just trying to get Terry Stokes into trouble when he came to see you the other day. I overheard them at Eddie's caravan this afternoon on my way to the library and he all but admitted it."

Monroe gave Penny a stern look. "Please tell me you're not conducting your own investigation, Penny?" he said with pleading exasperation. "You really need to leave this to us."

"I just overheard. I pulled over next to the field and witnessed raised voices through the hedge."

"And why did you need to stop next to that particular field?"

Penny thought about making an excuse. She could have spotted the red kite and wanted to make note for Mr Kelly. Fischer needed a walk. Something came loose in the back of the van and she had to stop and fix it. Any of those things sounded feasible to her ears, but she couldn't lie to John Monroe, so she opted for silence.

"Hmm." He said knowingly.

"There is some animosity between Tompkins and Stokes, John."

Monroe drained his glass and set it on the table. "I should have Tompkins arrested for wasting police time if that's the case. There's something particularly strange about that man. I'm new to the area so perhaps I can see it more objectively."

"No, he looks strange to all of us." Penny said.

Monroe smiled.

"Did you know they have some sort of land deal going on between them?" she continued.

"No, I didn't. What is it and how did you find out?"

"Susie did some digging. Apparently Eddie owns the land his caravan is on and him and Terry put in a planning application ages ago for houses. Eddie no longer wants to go ahead and the application time is running out. Terry still wants to push on with it. That's what they were arguing about when I heard them."

Monroe shook his head. "You know, I'm seriously thinking I should get you and Susie on the payroll as consultants or something. You both have a knack for finding out salient information." He took his phone out of his pocket. "Excuse me one minute while I pass this on and get someone to look into it further."

Penny finished her drink while waiting for him to complete his email.

"Right," he said, putting away his phone. "That's done. So, do you have plans for later? I wondered if you wanted to catch a film or something?"

Penny was about to agree when she remembered her arrangement with Susie. Even though she was sure her friend wouldn't mind the last minute cancellation, she would feel awful about it.

"Actually, I've arranged to meet Susie."

"Ah, another time then perhaps?"

"Actually, why don't you join us?"

Monroe looked unsure.

"It's the pub quiz at the Pig and Whistle. We keep losing to two teams that join quizzes all over the place. I think they are part of a semi-professional league but we're determined to beat them. At least once. You could join us, although we still haven't come up with a decent team name yet. What's your specialist subject?"

Monroe now looked worried.

"Specialist subject? This sounds quite serious. I don't think I have one, I like history. Sport maybe?"

"Great. Meet us at the Pig and Whistle around 7 o'clock. We usually have a drink first. How does that sound?"

Monroe nodded. "Yes, all right. I have a few things to finish off at the office first. I'll see you there."

They walked back to the car park, then went their separate ways. Penny watched him walk to his car, confident in his step, but not arrogant. She forced herself to stop staring and hopped into the driving seat, with Fischer scrabbling over her knee to get to his side.

On the way back, she noticed the red kite again and made a mental note to write it down when she got home. She couldn't stop, she had an outfit to sort out.

Once home, Penny gave Fischer his dinner and went for a shower, then went to find a suitable outfit.

Fischer sat on the end of the bed while she threw things haphazardly out of her wardrobe. Something smart, but not too smart. Glamorous? Did she actually own anything that could be described as glamorous? Maybe casual was the way to go. It was just the local pub on a Thursday night after all. But not something he'd seen her wearing before.

"I need your help, Fischer." She said to the little dog who was practically buried beneath her wardrobe detritus. "Do you think I should wear this?" It was a powder blue shirt with daisy design on the collar.

Fischer cocked his head to one side.

"No, I wore it on Monday, you're right. He'll notice that, he's a detective."

She rummaged some more and found a patterned blouse with tassels. "This one?"

Fischer cocked his head the other way.

"I know," she said, flinging it on a chair. "I've never liked that one either. I'll put it in the next charity bag that comes through the door. Should I wear jeans or a skirt? How about that dress, or is it too much for the pub?"

Fischer lay down and put his paw over his nose and whined.

Penny looked at the scattered clothes across her bed and sighed. She was being silly. She sat next to Fischer and gave him a hug. "Thank goodness you don't have to worry about clothes. Right, jeans it is. And this lightweight mustard jumper."

Fischer nuzzled her hand, and she gave him a kiss on the nose for being so patient. Almost dressed, she heard her phone buzz on the hall table. She looked at the bedside clock, twenty minutes to seven. The call was probably from Susie.

"Okay, time to go," she said, grabbing her denim jacket from the chair just in case.

She sent a quick text to Susie saying she was would be there soon, and that she was bringing a secret weapon.

The Pig and Whistle's claim to fame was as the oldest pub in the country and as such enjoyed the patronage of a lot of tourists as well as locals. The weekly quiz had been going for longer than Penny could remember. It was certainly well established when she'd returned to Cherrytree Downs after university.

Susie was standing at the bar with a large glass of wine in front of her when Penny and Fischer turned up. She gave Penny a hug and lifted Fischer for a cuddle, which had the dog wiggling in ecstasy.

"My round. What are you having? And what is this secret weapon?"

"You'll find out soon. I'll have the same as you, please. Are you in a party mood, Susie?"

"Why not? The kids are with their dad for a long weekend. He has great plans for them, so they'll have an excellent time. Swimming pool, water slides, you know the sort of thing. He always loved that stuff; he's like a big kid himself. So, I'm free." She raised her glass and took a sip.

Katie, the barmaid, put a second glass of white wine on the bar and Susie reached into her handbag for her purse.

"I'll get that." A voice said from behind them.

Penny turned to see John Monroe. He was still wearing the same shirt he'd worn at the Red Lion.

Susie gave Penny a look and mouthed, "Your secret weapon?"

Penny nodded briefly, and Susie grinned.

"Thank you, John."

"And a pint of the black stuff for me, please." He said to Katie.

"Good evening, Detective Inspector," Susie said with a cheeky smile.

"It's John this evening, Mrs Hughes."

"Susie."

"I hope I'm not late? I had to work on a bit longer than I expected. I've come straight from the station." He handed over a twenty pound note to Katie. "And one for yourself," he told her.

With everyone holding drinks, they made their way over to their regular table, close to the bar and the old stone inglenook fireplace. Fischer lay down next to a basket of logs by the side of the unlit fire and promptly fell asleep.

"So, did you come up with a better team name, Susie?" Penny asked.

Susie looked glum and shook her head. "Couldn't think of a thing. Anyway, with John here we need a moniker that will encapsulate something meaningful for all three of us."

"Actually," John said. "I hope I'm not speaking out of turn having just joined the team, but I've been thinking about that while I was at work. I might have something suitable."

"Go on." Susie and Penny both urged him. "What's your idea?"

"Well, it relates to books and reading," he said, gesturing at Penny. "Writing," nodding at Susie. "And two of the best detectives ever devised. One, a policeman," tapping his chest. "And the other an amateur sleuth," he finished with a pointed look at Penny, who laughed but also felt the heat rise in her face.

"Sounds perfect. What is it?" asked Susie.

"Agatha Quiztie."

Penny and Susie burst out laughing. "Oh, that's brilliant." Susie said, wiping tears of laughter from her eyes. "You deserve a pint after that little gem. The next one is on me."

"It is really good," Penny agreed. She was seeing a different John Monroe this evening, relaxed and less serious without the weight of the job on his shoulders. She very much liked what she saw.

As they reached the half way mark of the quiz, they realised they were doing really well as a team. Susie was having a great time, chatting and laughing and doodling on the sheet as she wrote down the answers. Penny had an excellent art and literature round and when John congratulated her on a perfect ten out of ten score, she felt herself glow. Or maybe it was just the wine. She returned the compliment as Monroe aced the picture round, identifying historic and geographical landmark images with ease.

"Are you going to answer any tonight?" Penny teased Susie.

"When we get to the round on bringing up children on a tight budget, I'm your gal." She laughed.

At the end of the night when the scores were announced they discovered they had come second, one point ahead of Artificial Intelligence. Universally Challenged were in the top spot, but they were only a few points behind them.

"Wow, that's the best we've ever done," Susie said, wide eyed and excited. "And all thanks to you, John."

"I wouldn't go that far. You two had as much input as me. Not to sound trite but it was a team effort."

Monroe finished his drink. Penny noticed he had slowly sipped the single pint throughout the evening, a sensible drinker.

"One more?" Susie asked, draining her own glass.

Penny was tempted. Spending more time with her best friend and Monroe in her favourite pub sounded lovely, but she was shattered and her bed was calling. She wanted to get back, brew a cup of fennel tea, and settle down with her book. She didn't have work the next morning, but she planned to take Fischer on a long walk over Sugar Hill to help him burn off some of the weight he'd gained from Susie's crispy treats.

"I'd love to, but I'm honestly too tired, Susie. I need to go home and sleep."

"I'll walk you back." Monroe said, standing up.

"The sensible crowd wins again," Susie said, slightly disappointed. "But I suppose I do have to work in the morning. The news doesn't write itself."

The evening sky was dramatic, a gibbous moon with a thick dark shadow over one quarter and iron grey clouds rolling across the moonlit sky. A breeze blew across the duck pond, creating ripples that lapped at the grassy bank.

Penny was glad she'd worn a jumper now and had had the foresight to bring her denim jacket at the last minute. She breathed in deeply, the cool air clearing her head.

Fischer pulled towards his favourite tree on the green.

"You go on," Penny said. "While I see to Fischer."

"We'll wait," Monroe said. "I'm not leaving you ladies alone so late at night."

Other customers were spilling out of the pub and heading off into the night, calling out their goodbyes as they went. The village was soon quiet again.

"Honestly, I'm fine. We'll catch you up."

"I insist. If there is a murderer on the loose, I can't in good conscience leave you alone."

Penny looked across the duck pond as Fischer finished his business, remembering the body of a friend, an old lady, had been found there. People could behave in the most unexpected and abhorrent ways and the idyllic village of Cherrytree Downs was not exempt from some of mankind's worst. Maybe John had a point.

Penny and Fischer walked back to where Susie and Monroe were waiting and they continued on to Penny's cottage, chatting amiably as they went.

"Penny has some of the best teas in the village, you know, if not all the downs. What say we have a cuppa to end the night?" Susie suggested.

"Yes, of course," Penny said. "It would be my pleasure."

Monroe smiled. "That sounds lovely. I'm quite partial to a cup of earl grey in the evening, if you have it?"

As Monroe followed Penny and Fischer through the gate and down the path, Susie called out goodbye.

"I've just remembered it's the early shift I'm on. You two have a lovely evening. Bye for now." She smiled brightly and turned away.

"Susie, wait. I thought you were coming in too?"

"I did too, Penny, but I really can't."

"Well, wait for John, you can't walk home by yourself." Penny said, turning to Monroe, "You don't mind, do you?"

"No, of course I don't. She shouldn't walk back alone."

"Honestly, it's not far," Susie protested. "I'll be fine. Nothing bad is going to happen to me in Cherrytree Downs."

"Wait, Susie," Penny said in a tone that brooked no argument.

Susie stopped with a sigh and a roll of her eyes. The plan she'd thought so clever backfiring spectacularly.

Monroe looked down at Penny. His collar was crumpled and his tie, taken off in the pub, was partially hanging out of his trouser pocket. He rubbed his chin, and Penny could hear the slight rasp. He needed a shave.

"On second thoughts, it's been a long day. Perhaps we can have that tea another time?"

Penny nodded, not trusting herself to speak. He gave her a quick peck on the cheek, bent down to say goodbye to Fischer, then turned on his heel in the direction of Susie.

Penny watched them walk down the lane together, then unlocked her front door.

"Well, that didn't quite go as Susie expected, did it, Fish Face?"

Fischer barked and trotted upstairs. Penny followed. Perhaps it was a good job in hindsight, because suddenly she could hardly keep her eyes open.

Nine

Penny awoke on Friday with renewed determination to find out what had happened to Mrs Sharp. There must be something she'd missed, but she couldn't think what it might be. She also remembered she hadn't told Monroe about her visit to Olive's house while they'd been in the pub the night before. But then again, there hadn't really been an opportune moment. He'd been so relaxed, they all had, and enjoying the evening without the responsibility of work. It was good to unwind and forget about the day job for a while. And what had she actually learned at the house? Nothing at all except that's where Terry had fitted the security door rather than at the shop.

As she walked Fischer down by the river, she mulled over her next course of action, and by the time she returned home her mind was made up. She'd go back to the house and see if there was something she'd missed. Mrs Sharp must have had a specific reason to have a security door fitted at her home. What had made her so worried? Had she been frightened about something? Concerned about unwanted visitors?

She bundled Fischer into the van and once more set off for Pikes Cross. Taking a right turn she continued down the road and turned in and parked where she had on her previous visit.

"Come on, Fish Face, let's see if we can get some answers this time."

She entered through the back gate, closed it, and let Fischer off his lead.

She again found it odd that all the curtains were closed downstairs. Had Mrs Sharp done that when she'd gone to work on Sunday morning? And if so, why? It would have made more sense to close them when she'd returned from work that evening. But of course, Penny thought sadly, she never did return. Surely she hadn't known what was going to happen to her?

She made her way round each of the ground-floor windows in turn, but couldn't see anything. She'd almost given up hope when she found the little window on the side, just off what she presumed to be the kitchen. It was the pantry and a small chink where the curtains didn't quite meet in the middle allowed her to see through to the room beyond. The pantry door was open and the small part of the kitchen she could see, was in disarray. Beyond that another open door revealed the edge of a piece of furniture, a bureau of some sort, tipped over and paperwork scattered everywhere.

Mrs Sharp was known to be a fastidious and tidy person, her shop was a testament to that. This was very much out of character and could only mean one thing; Mrs Sharp had been burgled. But what were they looking for? And more to the point, how did they get in?

Penny thought for a moment, then pulled out her phone. Reluctant as she was, she had to make a call.

When the phone was answered, it was the greeting she had expected.

"What do you want, Finch?"

Penny rolled her eyes.

"Charming, Terry. Do you answer the phone that way to all your customers?"

"Only the nosy ones. Now, I repeat, what do you want?"

"I want to find out who killed Mrs Sharp. You know it wasn't me who reported you to DI Monroe, it was Eddie Tompkins. He told you as much."

"See, you're a snoop, Finch, eavesdropping on private conversations."

"I happened to be walking my dog, Terry, that's all. Besides, you're still a suspect as far as the police are concerned. Did you know that?"

"I have an alibi. You know nothing."

"I know on-line gambling isn't a good alibi, Terry. Anyone could have access to your computer; it didn't have to be you.

Look, I'm not calling to argue with you, I want to help find who murdered Mrs Sharp and if you're innocent, then it would help clear your name if you'd help me."

There was a deathly silence at the other end of the phone, and Penny knew she had said too much. Not only had she broken the faith John had in her, she'd given away crucial private details of a murder enquiry to a potential murderer. But how else was she supposed to get Terry to help her if there wasn't something in it for him? It's how the Terry Stokes of the world worked. But she didn't really believe Terry was the murderer. Hadn't Mr Kelly told her at the beginning of the week Terry had shouted at Mrs Sharp that he wanted the money she owed him in his account by Monday? If that was the case then he wouldn't have killed her on the Sunday before she'd had a chance to pay him. It could be a double bluff, of course, but Penny didn't really think he had that sort of intelligence. But if Terry didn't do it, then who did? She waited, not wanting to interrupt while he thought about her request.

"All right, I'll help. I admit I shouted at her, but I didn't murder the old witch. What do you want from me?"

"It's about the security door you fitted. I thought it was at the shop."

"I never said it was at the shop."

"I know you didn't. Now I know it's at her house. Can you meet me there I need to get in somehow? I think someone's been in there that shouldn't have been."

"Broken in?"

"There's no sign of forced entry. I don't know how they got in if I'm honest."

On the other end of the line, Terry swore loudly.

"What is it, Terry?"

"I'll get the blame for this. It wasn't me but I'll get the blame."

"Why?"

"Because I've got the key."

It turned out when Terry had fitted the security door for Mrs Sharp, he'd handed over one of the two keys it came with but had left the other in his van. He couldn't find it in amongst the detritus, but promised he'd drop it in at the shop when he was passing. When Mrs Sharp didn't pay her bill, he decided to keep it until she did. Now, with her house being broken into and no sign of a forced entry, it wasn't looking good for Terry Stokes.

Penny met him at the garden gate.

"Here," he said, handing over the key. "I'm not coming in. The only thing I've done is fit the door. I've never been in the house so when your boyfriend comes looking for fingerprints he won't find any of mine. That'll prove I didn't break in."

It wouldn't, Penny thought. He could have been wearing gloves, but she didn't say so as he was already agitated enough.

"All right, can you stay and wait for me?"

"I'm not getting involved with this, Finch. It's nothing to do with me."

"I understand, Terry, and for what it's worth, I don't think you did it, but I need to get in there and I don't know what I'll find. Could you at least watch out for anything suspicious and help me if I call?"

Terry nodded gruffly, then got in his van, which he'd parked in the back lane, and folded his arms.

The gate was shut, so Penny left Fischer exploring the garden while she unlocked the door and went inside.

Even in the gloom caused by the closed curtains, it was obvious the entire house had been searched. The place was an absolute mess, with drawers upturned and contents scattered across the floor. Cupboard doors opened and the shelves roughly swept clear. Porcelain statues of shepherdesses holding sheep were smashed in the hearth and pictures taken from walls and left on the floor, glass smashed on some.

The walnut bureau she'd seen through the gap in the curtains earlier was on its side, surrounded by the accoutrements of what was obviously used as a writing desk; writing paper, notebooks, stamps, two glass paperweights with flowers inside frozen forever in time, and numerous pens and pencils alongside a brass letter opener.

Upstairs, the three bedrooms had had their beds stripped, and the bases overturned. Again drawers were emptied and thrown aside, as were the contents of the wardrobes. The bathroom hadn't fared any better. Towels in a heap in the bath and the cupboard above the sink laid bare. Pills and potions smashed and leaking in the basin.

She returned downstairs wondering if the burglar had found what he or she was looking for? Back outside, she found Terry still sitting in his van and Fischer digging just outside the door. Compared to the mess inside, a little misplaced earth was nothing, but she stopped him nonetheless.

"Fischer, stop that. Come here, good boy."

He trotted over, tail wagging furiously, and dropped a small muddy clump at her feet.

"What did you find, Fischer?"

She picked it up and brushing off the earth, found a cuff-link in the shape of a letter S.

"It must have belonged to Mr Sharp. Well done, Fish Face."

"Find anything?"

She looked up and saw Terry at the gate. She slipped the cuff-link in her pocket and, putting Fischer on his lead, went to meet him.

"No. The place has been searched thoroughly although I've no idea what they were looking for or if they found it. I have to call DI Monroe, Terry."

"Well, I'm not sticking around. Keep the key."

"Terry, if you leave now, it will only make you look more suspicious. I got in the house using a key you gave me, re-member. You need to give your side of the story. I'll back you up, tell them you helped me."

"Why would you do that? What's in it for you? You think you can hold it over my head in the future, is that it?"

"No, Terry, that's not it. Contrary to what you seem to believe, some people help for no other reason than they want to. To do what's right. I want to find the person who killed Mrs Sharp and considering you're the prime suspect at the moment I'd have thought you'd have wanted all the help you could get."

"Fine! I'll be in the van."

Penny shook her head. There was no pleasing some people. Taking out her phone, she called John Monroe directly. Her heart was beating ten to the dozen because she knew he'd be cross that she hadn't taken his advice to stay out of it. But on the other hand she'd found a second crime scene. Surely that was worth something?

"Penny, how are you?"

"I'm fine, thanks, and you?"

"Fine too. Busy with the case of course."

Pleasantries over Penny launched into the explanation of what she'd found and how she'd found it. There was a momentary silence and then DI Monroe told her to stay put, he'd be along shortly with the crime scene technicians.

"And tell Terry Stokes to stay there too. I'll need to take statements from you both."

Once the call had ended, Penny wandered over to give Terry the message then went and sat on Mrs Sharp's garden bench with Fischer to wait for the police.

Half an hour later, John Monroe appeared on foot and after a quick word with Terry Stokes made his way over to Penny. He sat next to her and reached down to scratch Fischer's ears.

"I can't keep you away from this, can I?"

"I'm sorry, John, it wasn't deliberate. I was wondering about the security door and drove around the back of the shop to see it for myself, except there wasn't one. I asked Mr Kelly, and he said Mrs Sharp lived here not above the shop like I'd thought."

"So you thought you'd come over and take a look?"

"Yes. As you can see, Terry fitted the door here, which makes me think she was afraid of something. And considering the place has been violently searched and Mrs Sharp is dead it would appear she was right to be frightened."

"And Terry had kept a key?"

"Yes. He was intending to return it to her though."

"Mmm."

"He refused to come in with me, saying his fingerprints will only be found on the door he fitted. He's never been inside the house. For what it's worth, I believe him. I know you have to investigate and find proof, but it seems too obvious for it to be Terry, just for the sake of a few hundred pounds for a door. He runs a business and wouldn't have many clients if he bumped them all off for late payment. Besides, if it was Terry that Mrs Sharp was afraid of she wouldn't have asked him to do the work would she? There were two keys to this door and Mrs Sharp will have had the other with her the night she was killed. I think the murderer took it and came here to look for something."

"All valid points, which I will bear in mind. Now, let's see what's inside before the team gets here, shall we? I assume you touched nothing?"

"Just the key and the door."

They wandered around the house together, Penny assuring the inspector everything was as she'd found it. Outside, he took her statement then did the same with Terry. He then announced they could both leave, but would need to come back to the station later in the day to sign their official statements.

"Will you let me know if you find anything?" Penny asked, as they watched Terry's van drive away.

"I'll come by your cottage later if that's all right with you?"

Penny nodded and walked back to the library van with Fischer. Pulling out onto the main road, she passed the crime scene van and wondered what they would find at the house. She hoped it would be something of import because she was beginning to lose hope the perpetrator would ever be found.

Ten

Penny had made a vegetable lasagna with garlic bread for her dinner, but there was enough for two if needed.

At seven o' clock, there was a knock at the door and Fischer ran down the hallway in excitement. It was John Monroe, a bottle of wine in his hand. At Penny's question he admitted he hadn't had time to eat and would welcome her invitation to dinner. Over the food and a glass of white wine he brought her up to date with what had been found at Mrs Sharp's home.

"Or more to the point, what we didn't find," he said.

"What do you mean? How would you know something was missing?"

"Mrs Sharp's Last Will. It was nowhere to be found."

"But wouldn't it have been kept by her solicitor or in the bank?"

"The original is with her solicitor. I've already been there and checked. But there was a copy she kept at her house, probably in the bureau. It's that one that's missing."

"So you know who will benefit from her death then?"

"I do. It's Chase Scarlett. Everything, the shop and business, the house and contents and everything else will come to her."

"Really? Does she know?"

"I would have thought so by now, yes. But she's in the clear as far as the murder is concerned. We're looking for someone else and so far, much to my frustration, they have managed to elude us."

"Its early days yet, John. Something will set you on the right track soon, I'm sure. Did you find anything else at the house?"

"Just a couple of letters from a developer offering to buy the shop. She'd written on them that she'd refused."

"Yes, it's well known she was the only one who was preventing the new building work going ahead. Are you looking into someone at the building company as a potential suspect?"

"We're looking into everything, Penny. But there's nothing on them so far and we can't place the owner or any of the staff at the scene. It's looking like a dead end, if you'll excuse the awful pun."

"And no sign of the secret recipe?"

John shook his head. "No. I expect she took that to her grave with her."

"What about fingerprints?"

"Yes, there were several, apart from Mrs Sharp's, which we are in the process of identifying now. They're at the top of the pile so I should have answers soon, assuming they are in the database."

Penny nodded and took the last bite of her lasagna before putting down her knife and fork and pushing the plate away.

"That was a lovely meal, Penny, thank you." John said as he finished his last bite.

"Would you like tea or coffee?"

"Coffee would be nice, thank you."

As Penny rose to fill the kettle, John's phone rang.

"DI Monroe. What? When? Where is she now? Right, I'm on my way."

He turned to Penny with a look of apology mixed with something else. Disappointment she thought.

"I'm sorry, I have to go. That was the station. Chase Scarlett has just been attacked."

On Saturday morning Penny was in the front garden putting the recycling in the bin when there was a call over the fence. It was Dorothy Walker.

"Dorothy, how lovely to see you. How was your holiday? You had good weather if that tan is anything to go by."

"It was fabulous, Penny. Sea, sand and Sangria, and plenty of sunshine. But it's good to be back home too. I must say I was surprised to see Chips Ahoy closed and in darkness. Olive is usually in there at the crack of dawn preparing for the busy weekend. Is she ill, do you know?"

"Oh, Dorothy, haven't you heard the news?"

"News? No, I've heard nothing. We only got back in the early hours this morning and went straight to bed for a few hours before I drove over here to get my new book from you. I haven't really seen anyone yet. Why, what's happened?"

Penny went on to explain how Mrs Sharp had died and that the police were still investigating to try to find the murderer. As expected Dorothy Walker was shocked.

"Penny, that's absolutely dreadful news. What a terrible thing to have happened. I can't quite believe it. Was it something to do with the car we saw at the back of the shop that night do you think?"

"What car, Dorothy?"

"We called for a taxi to take us to the airport; it's very expensive to leave the car in the airport car park for a week. It was very late on Sunday night and as you know we live at the back of Chips Ahoy. As we were getting in, I saw a large black vehicle parked under the trees at the side. I would have missed it except the taxi headlights caught it as we were leaving. I thought perhaps it was someone who'd gone to the pub and decided not to drive home after having one drink too many."

"Did you recognise it?"

"No, not at all. One large black land rover looks much the same as another doesn't it? Oh, it did have a sort of design on the back, in silver I think, like flames or something."

Penny frowned. She was sure she'd seen something like that recently but she couldn't remember where.

"Do you think I should tell the police, Penny?"

"Yes, I do. Here, I'll give you Detective Inspector Monroe's direct telephone number. He's in charge of the case. Tell him you got his number from me."

"Of course, thank you. Now, would it be too much of an imposition to get my book from the library? I know it's your day off."

"It's no problem at all. I put it to one side for you on Monday. Let me get the keys."

Penny went inside to get the van keys, her mind whirling as she tried to remember where she'd seen the car before. But try as she might, it just wouldn't come to her. Hopefully John would have more luck when Dorothy told him what she'd seen.

An hour after Dorothy had left with her new book and just as she was pulling on her boots to take Fischer for a long walk, John Monroe rang.

"Hello, John. Did Dorothy call you?"

"She did, that's partly why I'm ringing, to thank you."

"Do you know who the car belongs to?"

"Not at the moment, no, but when we find the owner it gives us additional ammunition for the case."

"I'm sure I've seen it before, I just can't remember where. I was about to take a long walk with Fischer to see if I can shake the information loose from my brain."

"Well, let me know as soon as you do."

"I will. So, how is Chase Scarlett?"

"She's fine, just understandably shaken."

"What happened?"

"She'd been to see the solicitor in Winstoke yesterday afternoon then decided to have a meal in town before getting the late bus back to Thatchings. Once she'd been released from custody, she'd made arrangements to go back and stay there for a while. Apparently she was jumped on her way to the bus stop and threatened. Whoever it was said someone would be in touch about selling the shop and she had to do exactly what they said or the next time she wouldn't get away so easily."

"Poor Chase. She must have been terrified. So this has all been about selling Chips Ahoy?"

"It's looking very much like it."

"And whoever broke into Mrs Sharp's house found the copy of her Will and knew Chase would inherit so threatened her?"

"Precisely."

"Where is she now?"

"Back at Thatchings, I had an officer drive her over there once she'd made her statement. She'll be safe until we find out who was responsible."

"Could she identify her attacker?"

"Unfortunately not. It was dark and he caught her from behind and dragged her into an alley at knife point. It was a male who had a distinctive smell, some sort of designer aftershave she thought. Apart from that she couldn't tell us any more except his rough height, he was quite tall, and weight, not too fat not too thin. Average really. Which quite honestly is so generic it could pertain to a lot of men in the area."

"Did she recognise the smell?" asked Penny as a sudden thought struck her.

"Hang on, I wrote it down."

Penny could hear the rustling of paper while John found his notes.

"Yes, here we are. Aniseed. It reminded her of those little purple sweet balls you used to buy by the ounce. Why?"

"Because I think I know what it is. It's Fennel. That's part of the recipe for Mrs Sharp's batter. Susie and her children have been feeding Fischer scraps recently, and he goes nuts every time he smells it. I spilled some new fennel tea the other day and his reaction was the same, that's what made me realise what it was. Whoever killed Mrs Sharp would likely have that smell about them if it's on their clothes. I think Chase Scarlett was attacked by the murderer himself, John."

John's parting comment before they ended the call was to tell her in no uncertain terms to forget any idea of pursuing the murder of Mrs Sharp. It was obvious they were dealing with a dangerous and quite probably deranged individual. Chase Scarlett was let go with a warning because she had something the killer wanted, Penny didn't and John was not prepared to be called out to another crime scene because something had happened to her.

She set out on her walk with Fischer, with John's concern ringing in her ears.

A break in the clouds appeared overhead as she sauntered out of Cherrytree Downs onto the footpath which would lead her over the shoulder of Sugar Hill. It was beautiful, peaceful and relaxing and she felt the warmth on her face before the clouds once more covered the sun and a gust of wind brought rain blowing over the fields, splattering against her raincoat and flecking her jeans a darker blue.

She thought about what John had said as she walked and knew he only had her best interests at heart. She was a librarian for goodness' sake, what was she doing chasing a murderer all over Hampsworthy Downs? She loved nothing more than a good mystery to pit her wits against but realistically by investigating a real life crime she could only damage a serious police investigation, no matter how much help she thought she was giving. If she made one wrong move the killer could get away, or worse she could be hurt. No, perhaps it was time to hang up her proverbial deerstalker and leave the investigation to the police. She'd been lucky twice before but three times would certainly be pushing it.

"What do you think, Fish Face? No more investigations, agreed?"

The happy little Jack Russell trotting along beside her looked up, tongue lolling from his mouth in a canine smile.

Before she knew it Penny was entering the village of Rowan Downs, they'd walked almost a mile and a half even with the short-cuts she knew. Despite the intermittent rain, it was busy in the village as the local shops had everything you could possibly want without the need to travel into Winstoke town. The green grocer, butcher and baker had queues out of their doors and the old newsagent was throng with children wanting to buy sweets. It sold the largest selection of what was now termed retro sweets in the county. Bought by the ounce and sold in pink and white striped paper bags. In the window large glass jars made a colourful display, tempting everyone who went passed, and Penny was no exception.

From cola cubes, fruit salads and black jacks, to Edinburgh rock, sour apples and lemon sherbets, there was something to suit everyone. Penny was torn between sherbet pips and Edinburgh Rock, but finally opted for a couple of ounces of the latter.

As she left the shop, Fischer gave a little bark and looked up at her with a hopeful expression.

"No, these aren't for you, Fischer," Penny said, popping a sweet in her mouth. "But I do have something for you."

She delved into her pocket and brought out a meaty treat for her little friend, who wolfed it down.

She continued along the pavement towards the junction with the road that led towards Winstoke, carefully checking both ways before crossing and carried on along the opposite side of the village. She was dipping into her confectionery bag, trying to decide on what flavour to have next, when she nearly collided with a man standing outside Chips Ahoy.

Eleven

"Oh, excuse me. I do apologise. I wasn't looking where I was going," Penny said in a conciliatory but cheery tone. She looked up and was about to offer the man a sweet when she found herself staring into the sneering face of Simon Snipe.

"Watch where you're going, you ignorant woman," Snipe said unpleasantly. "You nearly knocked me into the road. What if a car had been coming? Not that there's much traffic in this pathetic little backwater." He looked back at the Chips Ahoy building.

Fischer tugged at his lead and lunged towards Snipe. Standing on his hind legs, he stuck his nose up the sleeve of Snipe's jacket. Snipe jerked his arm away, shouting a curse that echoed down the quiet street and placed his foot against the little dog's ribs, pushing him away sharply. Penny pulled Fischer towards her in shock.

"How dare you kick my dog!" she shouted. Utterly appalled that anyone would do such a thing.

Snipe curled his lip. "I didn't kick him, I just shoved the mangy little mutt with my foot. If you could keep control of your animal, then I wouldn't have to. Don't look at me like that," he scoffed. "I'll give you and your nasty little dog something to be upset about in a minute."

Penny found herself at a loss for a suitable comeback. She wanted to tell Snipe exactly what she thought of him, but couldn't find the words. She decided it would be better to say nothing. She didn't care if he turned on her but she would not risk Fischer getting hurt. She stepped around him, determined to finish her walk before turning and heading home. She tucked the bag of sweets in her pocket. They had suddenly lost their flavour.

As she stepped away Fischer once more lurched for Snipe, but Penny knew he was not being vicious. He was smiling and excited. He shoved his nose in Snipe's cuff again, and the odious man jerked away as though he'd been bitten.

"Fischer, stop it. Leave the man and his sleeve alone." She pulled him back towards her and kept a tight hold on his lead.

Snipe kicked out at Fischer, missed, and came forward again, determination etched on his face as he pulled back his leg ready to give a savage kick to the little dog. Fischer avoided the swinging shoe and bounded forward on hind legs, once more determined to get to the man's sleeve. Snipe backed away, hands held high.

"Get that crazy dog away from me! What's the matter with you? This place is full of nut jobs. Crazy old ladies, maniac dogs and crumbling old buildings. As soon as I have that old shop," he spat, waving a hand at Chips Ahoy, "I'll pull it down and build modern apartments. It'll bring in proper, decent, wealthy people and get rid of scum like you."

Snipe stormed off with Fischer valiantly trying to tear after him, but Penny had a tight hold. She'd never seen Fischer so single minded. Dogs could usually sense when someone didn't like them and stayed out of the way. Fischer was usually no exception but for some reason he wanted to get close to Snipe, even though it was obvious he hated the little dog. So why was he so keen on Snipe? What was it about his jacket? He'd been the same when they'd met in Edward's office a few days before.

She looked up at the closed Fish and Chip shop. The murder of Mrs Sharp was dreadful and what John had told her about the batter going everywhere during the struggle was playing like an echo in her mind. The batter that was flavoured with fennel. The ingredient that her little dog seemed to have become addicted to.

The realisation hit Penny like a wet fish across the face. She saw a black jeep with silver flames decorating the rear wheel arches accelerate away and turn onto the Winstoke road.

She pulled out her phone and called John Monroe. It went straight to answer phone. *Of all the times not to answer his phone*, Penny thought. She left an urgent message, then called

Susie. She needed to get to Winstoke urgently, but her van was a mile and a half away.

"Susie owes us a lift, Fischer."

She called her friend's number, but another answer phone message played in her ears. With both her parents and Mr Kelly unavailable, there was no choice but to run back home and get her van. Wherever Snipe was going in such a hurry was obviously important to the case. She only hoped she'd make it in time.

She made one final call to a local taxi company in Winstoke but with an estimated time of half an hour before it would arrive, everybody wanted taxis now the weather had turned. She would be better trying to make it home.

"Come on, Fish Face, we're going to have to run for it. Wherever Snipe is going, it must be to get rid of evidence, he must have realised why you're so interested in him."

It was a mile and half back to Cherrytree Downs along the footpath, Penny set off at a brisk run through the village. She made it to the old timber stile that would put her on the footpath in seconds. She could see the rooftops of her home village just over the shoulder of Sugar Hill. She felt the wind at her back propelling her forward, her boots swishing through the damp grass. She unclipped Fischer's lead and let the little dog run.

"Stay with me Fischer, your four legs can go a lot faster than my two," she panted.

The sky was dark overhead, with huge towering clouds the colour of bruises. Somewhere in the distance, Penny heard a rumble of thunder. It rolled on for a full fifteen seconds. To the south there was a storm raging and with the wind at her back she knew it was headed her way.

As she ran, she unzipped her jacket, feeling her body heat up from the exertion. The rain on her face mixing with the sweat on her brow. Another rumble of thunder, nearer this time, and Penny saw a flash of light in the clouds above.

"It's getting closer, Fischer. We really don't want to be caught out in the open when the storm hits."

Penny pushed herself to run faster. She was not a sprint athlete by any stretch of the imagination. A gentle walk was more her style and in fact she could walk for hours around the Hampsworthy Downs. But this was a different ball game entirely. She still had a mile to go to reach Cherrytree Downs, and even at her fastest knew it would take at least another twenty minutes. She was fit and healthy, but not fast. She wasn't built for running and she felt the breath burning in her chest as she put one foot determinedly in front of the other, pounding the footpath.

Fischer was enjoying the run, his little legs throwing him forward with no effort. Penny tried to keep pace with him, but there was no way she could match the little dog for either speed or stamina. All she could do was pray and keep moving, trying to get to her van as quickly as possible. With less than a quarter of a mile to go, she felt for the keys in her pocket. The rain started to lash down in huge sheets driven by the wind. The thunder grew louder, and she felt as though it were chasing her. The hair on her arms was beginning to stand on end and she could smell the sharp, fresh, pungent aroma of ozone, almost taste it.

At last she ran into the village, the soft grass now gone, changed for the paving slabs of Cherrytree Downs. She thundered along toward her little cottage, her boots heavy, her skin flushed, perspiration soaking her clothes from the inside as rain soaked them from without.

The streets were empty, everyone indoors sheltering from the storm. The thunder exploded over her head. The sky lit up with a sudden flash, and Penny felt the hair on the back of her neck stand up in response.

She got the van keys ready and came breathlessly to the driver's side door. Unlocking the van, she waited for Fischer to jump into his seat then pulled off her wet jacket, flinging it into the passenger foot-well as she climbed in. She fired up the engine and switched on the windscreen wipers. Time to catch a murderer.

Penny drove out of Cherrytree Downs and onto the stretch to Rowan Downs. There she took a left onto the main Winstoke road and was able to pick up speed. She raced past Tompkins'

field and saw the man himself standing bare chested in the middle of the expanse of grass, arms outstretched and face turned upwards, letting the rain wash over him.

The rain also washed over the road in front of Penny's van. It slashed against the windscreen and the wipers were struggling to keep the view clear. She was forced to slow down to prevent getting into an accident, ever mindful that she was chasing a killer and she could already be too late.

As she approached the town limits, she slowed to a crawl, a careful twenty miles per hour, all the while scanning the side streets for Snipe's car. Then she saw it.

"There, Fischer! Outside the Nice n' Easy dry cleaners."

She parked the van in the first available space; a little further down and on the opposite side of the road to Snipe's car. She opened the door and jumped down to the pavement, Fischer trotting eagerly at her side.

As they entered the dry cleaners, she saw Snipe hand his jacket over the counter. She unclipped Fischer's lead.

"Get it, Fischer!" Penny yelled, and the little dog jumped onto the counter and grabbed the jacket, snarling and tugging. The woman behind the counter let go in shock and Penny dashed forward, grabbing the jacket and calling Fischer to heel.

"Call the police," she said to the worried girl behind the counter. "Ask for DI Monroe and tell him it's Penny Finch who needs him."

She turned back to Snipe, who made a grab for his jacket and turned it into a tug of war.

"You're crazy! Let go of my jacket this instant."

"No. This is evidence, Mr Snipe. Proof you killed Mrs Sharp."

The young girl behind the serving counter, having made her call to the police station, stepped back totally bemused and unsettled by the fight happening in the usually quiet dry cleaners. A rumble of thunder overhead shook the tall windows in their frames, and a flash of lightening lit up Snipe's face as he snarled at Penny. Fischer was dancing around their feet, barking excitedly and jumping up to try to reach the jacket.

Snipe pulled the jacket hard and the surprise move and momentum brought Penny with it. She almost lost her footing on the wet floor, but her heavy walking boots saved her from falling. Fischer gave another jump and managed to secure his teeth on the jacket's cuff, growling through a mouthful of cloth. Snipe growled back and lashed out with a swinging back hand that caught poor Fischer a stinging blow on the side of his head.

As Fischer let go of the jacket and dropped to the floor with a yelp, Penny felt her blood boil. She had never known herself to feel real anger before, but when she saw Fischer stagger after a blow from Snipe she felt pure white hot fury rise in her. She gave the jacket an almighty pull with all her strength and freed it from Snipe's grasp.

"You won't get away with it, Snipe. Cleaning this jacket will wash away the evidence that you were the one who murdered poor Olive Sharp. You held her down and drowned her in vat of batter. The one with the secret ingredient that Fischer likes so much and could smell on your cuffs. You may have tried to wash it off, but Fennel lingers and is difficult to get rid of completely. I'm sure the police forensics team will be able to find the traces they need to put you away for good. You are a murderer, Simon Snipe, the lowest of the low, and you are going to answer for your crime."

Snipe darted forward and grabbed for his jacket, his knuckles white as his fingers clawed the material. Penny looked at his hands and had no trouble imagining them holding down Olive Sharp.

Snipe tugged again and ripped the jacket from Penny's grasp. She winced as she felt a fingernail break. Then with a snarl he reached for her shirt, fingernails scraping her neck and leaving angry red welts.

"You interfering, meddling, cow," he hissed, shoving her backwards. She stumbled, but once again her sturdy boots kept her from falling. Fischer was dancing and snapping at Snipe's ankles, but Penny called him away and held onto him before he could receive another kick. Snipe bundled up his jacket and, holding it tightly, turned to leave the shop.

Just as Snipe reached the door, it was flung open. The shop bell tinkled, but was drowned out by a powerful rumble of thunder, and a flash of lightening lit up the figure of John Monroe standing in the doorway.

"Stop right there, Mr Snipe."

"His jacket," Penny said breathlessly. "It's got batter on the cuffs. Mrs Sharp's batter. The fennel won't wash out."

Monroe looked at Penny, then back at Snipe. "You're under arrest for the murder of Mrs Olive Sharp. Detective, take him away."

A young detective stepped in past Monroe and, handing his boss the bunched up jacket, put handcuffs on Simon Snipe and led him away reciting the police caution. As thunder rumbled in the distance, Snipe turned and looked back, his eyes filled with hatred and his lip curled in a vicious snarl directed at Penny.

Penny felt a shiver as Snipe held her gaze, but her view of him was suddenly blocked as Monroe stepped forward.

"Penny, what did I say about not getting involved?"

Then, noticing the scratches on her neck and the fact she was shaking from the shock of having just had a fight with a murderer, he realised this was not the best time for a reprimand. He took her gently in his arms for a moment, feeling her lean into him, then guided her towards the door.

"Come on, I'll take you home."

He clipped Fischer's lead to his harness and walked them both out of the shop to his car. Once settled, he went back to speak with one of his officers who was taking a witness statement from the shaken shop girl. Penny watched him ask the girl a couple of questions, nodding while he took notes. He returned to them a few minutes later.

Twelve

The three of them sat in silence on the way back to Cherrytree Downs. Fischer settled on Penny's knee and fell asleep, twitching every so often as he no doubt relived his attack on Simon Snipe's jacket. Or perhaps he was just chasing rabbits in his dreams.

Monroe had put his coat around her shoulders and turned the car heater on full, but still she shivered.

Behind them one of John's officers was driving her library van, and behind him another officer was following to take him back to Winstoke. Penny didn't even remember handing over her keys.

John drove carefully. The freak summer storm, having now passed over, was rumbling away to the North and the rain had slowed to a steady persistent drizzle. The windscreen wipers swished in large lazy strokes, clearing the glass and showing the countryside ahead. Penny saw the red kite circling over

Sugar Hill as they moved closer to Cherrytree Downs. It seemed a lifetime ago since she'd first saw her and stopped in the lay-by to make a note for Mr Kelly.

Eventually, they pulled up outside her cottage. John thanked his officers and saw them on their way, then unlocked her door and guided her to the kitchen where he sat her at the kitchen table and put the kettle on.

"Perhaps you ought to change out of those wet clothes, Penny? I'll have tea waiting for you."

Once she was back in the kitchen clad in warm dry clothes, a steaming cup of tea in front of her, she and Monroe discussed the apprehension of Simon Snipe.

"So it was clever young Fischer who put you onto Simon Snipe, was it?"

"Yes, it was eventually. Although to be honest, I was a bit slow on the uptake. Susie had been feeding him chip shop scraps like I told you before. It must be the equivalent of catnip for felines. Snipe's accountant is Edward, did you know that?"

Monroe shook his head.

"Well, he was there the day I returned Edward's book, and Fischer was licking his jacket before we went in. Then he couldn't keep away from him while we were in there. I couldn't work it out because Fischer always knows when he's not welcome. When he's dealing with someone who doesn't like dogs, like Snipe, he stays away from them. I parked next to his car that day too. That's where I'd seen it before when Dorothy mentioned it to me, but again I didn't put two and two together until it was almost too late."

Monroe shook his head and took a sip of tea.

"It wasn't too late. You caught him, Penny. But what on earth were you thinking chasing after him like you did? You could have been hurt."

"The only thing I was thinking of was the fact he was most likely going to dispose of some sort of evidence, and I was right. His jacket cuffs were stained with fennel flavoured batter which put him at the scene of the crime. I was surprised I got there in time actually considering I had to run home to get the van from Rowan Downs and then drive to Winstoke."

"I had a brief chat with the girl at the dry cleaners before we left. Saturday is their busiest day and there was a queue of other customers before Snipe. If you'd arrived five minutes later, you'd have missed him."

They were interrupted by the ping of Monroe's phone. He glanced at the text message, and Penny saw a smile creep across his face as he read it. He looked up at her with a grin.

"We've got him. That was the forensics lab. There was an unidentified fingerprint at Chips Ahoy and two at Mrs Sharp's house, again unidentified but the same as the one at the shop. All the prints have just been confirmed as belonging to Simon Snipe."

"What about her Will?"

"I have my men searching both his house and work premises and his vehicle. If he's the one that took it, and it seems very likely, then we'll find it."

"Oh, I've just remembered. Fischer found something."

Penny got up and went to rummage in the pocket of her coat. She came back and dropped something in Monroe's outstretched hand.

"A cuff-link?"

"Yes. It's in the shape of a letter 'S' as you can see. Fischer dug it up just outside the door of Mrs Sharp's house. I thought it must have belonged to Mr Sharp and been there a while, but it could easily be 'S' for Snipe, couldn't it?"

Monroe reached down and rubbed Fischer's head. "Well done again, Fischer. I think we need to make you an official Police Dog." He turned back to Penny. "If this does belong to Snipe, then we'll find the matching one. It's all the more proof that he was there and every bit of evidence will help find him guilty. If it doesn't belong to him then I'll give it back to Chase Scarlett. By rights it is hers now."

Before John left to go back to the station to oversee the questioning and official charges to be brought against Simon Snipe, Penny asked if he would like to come to Sunday lunch the next day.

"Yes, I would like that very much. Thank you."

"Would you mind terribly if I asked Susie too? The children are away at the moment, so she's on her own. And now Mrs Sharp's murder has been solved she's going to want to report on it. Perhaps it would be better if you were there to approve what she'll want to print so it doesn't jeopardise your case?"

John laughed. "Well, here's hoping she'll listen to me. But no, of course I don't mind. Until tomorrow then."

All signs of the storm the day before had gone when Penny awoke on Sunday morning and summer was back in full force. She set up the table, chairs and a large umbrella on the small patio in the back garden, ready for lunch.

At one o'clock the bell rang and Fischer darted to the door, claws clicking on the floor as he danced. It was Susie.

She greeted Penny with a huge hug, then stood back, a look of concern etched on her face.

"Are you all right?"

"Yes, I'm fine now, don't worry. Come on through, I've set lunch up on the patio. John should be here soon."

"Penny, I am so sorry I wasn't able to drive you yesterday. I didn't pick your message up until it was all over."

"You told me that last night when I invited you to lunch. Honestly, Susie, it's fine. Please, stop worrying."

Ten minutes later John arrived and twenty minutes after that they were sitting outside under the shade of the umbrella, a Penny style Sunday lunch set out before them.

"So has Snipe confessed?" Susie asked between mouthfuls of nut roast.

John shook his head and reached for the wine, topping up their glasses.

"You would have thought with all the evidence stacked against him he would have. But no, he's denying any involvement. We'll prove otherwise of course."

"So, this shady business that Eddie Tompkins and Terry Stokes were involved in. Have you found out any more?" Penny asked.

"One of my sergeants found out about it early this morning."

"You've got them working on a Sunday?" Susie said.

"There's no rest for the police, Susie. Besides, I'm a slave driver, didn't you know?"

They laughed. If any boss was the antithesis of a slave driver, it was John Monroe.

"So what did he find out?"

"Apparently, Terry had a verbal agreement with Snipe to purchase his share of the land that he and Eddie own jointly."

"The field?"

John nodded. "The field. But Snipe's buying of it came with a few stipulations. Mainly that Eddie agreed to the development of the land, which of course he didn't. It was in Terry's interest to try to persuade Eddie because not only would Terry get a lump sum for his share, he would also get a large and potentially very lucrative building contract out of it. One that would set him up financially for a long time."

"When I was at the accountants, I overheard a conversation between Edward and Snipe. It sounded as though Snipe's company was in danger of going under. How could he have afforded to pay for Terry's share of the land?" Penny asked, taking a sip of wine.

"I think it was a case of robbing Peter to pay Paul," John said. "There's no doubt he was in over his head, mortgaged to the hilt. But if the development had gone ahead then he would, as the saying goes, have been *'quids in.'* Unfortunately Eddie was in the way."

"You mean he was in danger?" Susie said.

"I have no doubt about it. The agreement Eddie and Terry had was that should something happen to one of them, the other would automatically get their share. So in effect would own the whole plot. I suspect it would only have been a matter of time before I was called out to a second fatal crime scene."

"And poor Mrs Sharp was killed purely so the development could go ahead on her plot and expand over the adjacent field, which would make it worth far more?"

"That's the crux of it, Susie, yes. Just pure greed." John confirmed.

Penny rose and began to clear away their empty plates ready for desert. It was a new vegan recipe she was trying, a sumptuous Raspberry Cheesecake with a creamy lemon layer and a toasty walnut crust. Alongside she served a three ingredient vegan ice cream. It went down a storm with her guests, neither of whom could believe it was vegan. Over coffee, Penny asked about Mrs Sharp's Will.

"Did you find it?"

"We did indeed. It was in the glove compartment of Snipe's car. Alongside three very nasty threatening letters he'd penned to Mrs Sharp demanding she sell him the business and the building. He obviously stole those at the same time he stole the Will as he knew they'd implicate him."

"In his car? What a ridiculous place to put them." Penny said, astounded.

John shrugged. "That was the arrogance of the man. He never thought he'd be caught. We also found the burnt remains of the clothing he wore when he strangled Olive Sharp in his garden. Strange he didn't burn the jacket too. It must have been a favourite. Arrogant, and didn't expect to be caught like I said."

"Well, he didn't count on super sleuths Finch and Fischer, did he?" Susie said with a grin.

At four thirty, Susie bid them both goodbye and thanked Penny profusely for a fabulous lunch.

"The kids are due home at five, and I have an article to write for the morning edition. Thanks John for all the information. Look out for it tomorrow, you'll both be mentioned as well as the star of the show, Fischer Finch!"

"Woof!"

Once Susie had gone over tea in the garden John said his piece.

"I don't mean to sound harsh, Penny, but I did ask you not to get involved with this murder. You put yourself in danger. Snipe is more than just a property developer. He is a killer. He killed Olive Sharp in the most brutal way and I have no doubt he would have killed Tompkins eventually too. You had him cornered in that shop and he was desperate and vicious enough to have done you real physical harm."

"I called everyone I could think of, John, including you, before I went after him. I couldn't let him get away, could I? You didn't answer."

"My phone went to voice mail because I was working, putting together the final pieces of evidence so we could arrest him. Please, can I ask that you don't do anything like this again?" he said, taking her hand. "I'm just worried about your safety."

Penny nodded. "I'll do my best."

They sat like that, chatting companionably for a further hour before John had to leave.

"I still have a few loose ends to tie up. If not before, perhaps we could meet at the Pig and Whistle on Thursday? We have a score to settle with Universally Challenged."

Penny grinned. "That sounds perfect. I look forward to it."

"Oh, there is just one other thing I'd like to run by you."

"Yes?"

"Well, as you know, PC Bolton has now left and moved away. It means the property will be put on the market, there's no room in the budget to maintain a police house these days. I'm thinking of putting in an offer."

"Oh. Well, Cherrytree Downs is a lovely village. I'm sure you'll be very happy here and it would be nice to have you as a neighbour."

"So you wouldn't mind?"

"Mind? No of course not."

"That's settled then. I'll get the ball rolling tomorrow." He said with a grin.

Penny saw Monroe off, standing by her front door. She watched him drive into the distance then looked down at Fischer, sitting happily at her feet.

"I think we can chalk up another win for Fischer and Finch on this one, don't you think, little man?"

Fischer let out a yap of agreement and Penny gently closed her cottage door, thinking how lovely it would be if John were living close by.

All week long, throughout the villages and hamlets of Hampsworthy Downs, the talk at the mobile library was only of the death of Mrs Sharp and how the property developer Simon Snipe was responsible. Thanks to Susie's article in the Winstoke Gazette, Penny and Fischer were congratulated wherever they went as being instrumental in the capture of the murderer.

The days were long, bright and warm, and Penny enjoyed every one of them. On Thursday Mr Kelly, back from his short holiday, burst into the library excited and breathless.

"The red kite, Penny. The chicks have fledged. All three of them. You should see them, Penny; they're all nesting in Cringle Wood. I expect they will spread out before long and we'll see them all around the downs. It's so exciting that she actually raised a full, healthy brood."

"That's wonderful news, Mr Kelly. Do you want to stay and have a cup of tea with me to celebrate?"

"Any other time I would say yes, but I'm meeting Laura shortly, we're going for a fish and chip supper later. I suppose you've heard that Chips Ahoy has reopened?"

"But will it be the same without a Sharp at the helm?"

"But there will be, Penny. It's the sister Chase Scarlett, the famous actress. They say she's putting her own twist on the famous recipe. We're not sure if it will be as good, but Laura and I are going to find out."

Mr Kelly departed with a wave, beaming for joy and with a spring in his step, excited that the red kite was once more established in the downs and that his favourite chip shop was once again open for business.

That evening, as she drove home from Winstoke, Penny stopped in Rowan Downs and decided to pay a visit to Chips Ahoy. She could already see from across the road the queue meandering out of the door and along the pavement. As she reached the corner Susie and her children stepped out of the shop with a bag of chips and scraps each. Sam and Ellen immediately bending down to make a fuss of Fischer.

"Penny, I know these aren't your thing, but they are truly better than ever. I'm so happy Chase decided to reopen the shop. So, how are you doing? Are we still on for tonight?"

"I'm fine, Susie, thanks, and yes, John and I will meet you at the pub later. I really think we stand a good chance of winning this week."

Susie edged closer and dropped her voice. "So, are you and John an item now?"

Penny grinned. "I'm not sure. Possibly. We get on well together. I'm taking it slowly and seeing where it goes."

Susie leaned in for a hug. "Very sensible. I'm really pleased for you. He's a good man and you deserve someone who will treat you properly. Right, I'd better go. See you later."

As Susie left, Chase Scarlett exited the shop and met her on the pavement, a sausage wrapped in greaseproof paper in her hand.

"Penny, I owe you a debt of gratitude for bringing Simon Snipe to justice. Well, you and your wonderful dog." She held up the sausage. "A reward for the little hero. Would that be all right with you?"

Fischer looked up at Penny, tongue out, smiling excitedly. How could she deny him a sausage for all his hard work?

"What do you say, Fischer?"

"Woof."

"Oh, he is just delightful." Chase said as Fischer shook hands and gently took the sausage from her.

"So you're planning on staying in Rowan Downs, Chase?"

"I am indeed. I have great plans for the shop, it's the least I can do to keep my dear brother- and sister-in-law's memories alive. As you can see I have already taken on a manager," she said pointing inside where a young man was busy serving customers. "I poached him from a shop in Winstoke. And I intend to open the upstairs as a cafe and restaurant."

"It looks as though it will be a great success.' Penny said, indicating the queue, which if anything had grown larger since she'd arrived. "I assume you found the secret recipe?"

"No need. Between you and me, I've always known it. It was my mother's recipe. My brother and I grew up with it and it will always remain in the family. I do have some ideas to improve upon it though."

"Well, I hope you'll be very happy here in Rowan Downs."

"I certainly will be. I don't know how I can ever thank you for saving both me and the shop from that dreadful developer. And if it doesn't sound too cheeky, perhaps I can ask another favour from you, Penny?"

"I'll help if I can."

"I've been asked to become director of the local amateur dramatics society, and am looking for a play for our first production. As the local librarian I thought you'd be able to find something suitable for me?"

"I'm sure I can help with that. I'll do some digging and let you know. I'll drop your library card application in on Monday when I'm in the village."

Ms Scarlett bid Penny and Fischer adieu before returning inside to her customers, and Penny and Fischer jumped in the van to drive back to Cherrytree Downs.

"Now, what shall I wear tonight, Fischer?"

Fischer whined and put his paw over his nose, and Penny laughed.

"I'm only joking, Fischer, it doesn't matter what I wear. For once, I have a man who is interested in me for who I am and not what I look like."

Penny concentrated on her driving, looking forward to a night out with friends after another lovely week.

If you enjoyed *Battered to Death*, the third book in the Finch & Fischer series, please leave a review on Amazon. It really does help and you'd make the author very happy.

About the Author

J. New is the author of ***THE YELLOW COTTAGE VINTAGE MYSTERIES***, traditional English whodunits with a twist, set in the 1930's. Known for their clever humour as well as the interesting slant on the traditional murder mystery, they have all achieved Bestseller status on Amazon.

J. New also writes two contemporary cozy crime series:

THE TEA & SYMPATHY series featuring Lilly Tweed, former newspaper Agony Aunt now purveyor of fine teas at The Tea Emporium in the small English market town of Plumpton Mallet. Along with a regular cast of characters, including Earl Grey the shop cat.

THE FINCH & FISCHER series featuring mobile librarian Penny Finch and her rescue dog Fischer. Follow them as they dig up clues and sniff out red herrings in the six villages and hamlets that make up Hampsworthy Downs.

Jacquie was born in West Yorkshire, England. She studied art and design and after qualifying began work as an interior designer, moving onto fine art restoration and animal portraiture before making the decision to pursue her lifelong ambition to write. She now writes full time and lives with her partner of twenty-two years, her dog, Oscar and seven cats, all of whom she rescued.

If you would like to be kept up to date with new releases from J. New, you can sign up to her *Reader's Group* on her website www.jnewwrites.com You will also receive a link to download the free e-book, *The Yellow Cottage Mystery*, the short-story prequel to The Yellow Cottage Vintage Mystery series.